VESNA

WAITING FOR A PARTY

CROMER

PUBLISHED BY SALT PUBLISHING 2024

2 4 6 8 10 9 7 5 3 1

First published in Great Britain in 2024 by
Salt Publishing Ltd
12 Norwich Road, Cromer, Norfolk NR27 0AX

www.saltpublishing.com

Salt Publishing Limited Reg. No. 5293401

A CIP catalogue record for this book is available from the British Library

ISBN 978 1 78463 322 6 (Paperback edition)
ISBN 978 1 78463 323 3 (Electronic edition)

Typeset in Neacademia by Salt Publishing

Printed and bound in Great Britain by Clays Ltd, Elcograf S.p.A

VESNA MAIN was born in Zagreb, Croatia, where she studied Comparative Literature, before obtaining a PhD in Elizabethan Studies from the Shakespeare Institute at the University of Birmingham. She later worked as a journalist, lecturer and arts administrator.

Her published fiction includes a short story collection, *Temptation* (Salt, 2018), a novel-in-dialogue, *Good Day?* (Salt, 2019), which was shortlisted for the Goldsmiths prize, an autofiction, *Only A Lodger . . . And Hardly That* (Seagull Books 2020), and a novella, 'Bruno and Adèle' in *Shorts III* (Platypus Press, 2021). Two of her stories are published in *Best British Short Stories* (Salt 2017, 2019); many others have appeared in journals in print and online.

In her writing, Main is interested in telling stories in ways that explore and extend the boundaries of the narrative genre.

ALSO BY VESNA MAIN

NOVELS

A Woman with no Clothes On (Delancey Press, 2008)

The Reader the Writer (Mirador, 2015)

Good Day? (Salt, 2019)

Only A Lodger . . . And Hardly That (Seagull Books, 2020)

SHORT STORIES

Temptation: A User's Guide (Salt, 2018)

For Milo and Phoebe,

hoping your world is better
than the world we have now

WAITING FOR A PARTY

YES. SHE REMEMBERS the full moon, a large, luminescent paper collage against the sky, the fuliginous sky. That was the word he used, the word that stuck with her. She remembers the sharp lines of the full moon. Later, the image made her think of a picture drawn by a child, with the sky's sootiness, threatening, noxious, replaced by dark navy blue, and a sprinkling of scintillating stars. She doesn't remember there being stars on the night, but they entered her memory at some point and remained. That image, the transformed image of the view from the car parked to the side of Petersham Road, became associated with the man. But despite what the symbolism of the moon might suggest, she doesn't remember him as cold and changeable. Perhaps he was but she could not tell at the time, nor could she tell that later but, if pushed, she would read the connection between him and the image that stood for him in her mind as implying art, meaning artfulness, artificiality, even affectedness, and play, as in lack of seriousness, unpredictability, randomness. Ultimately, he remained an enigma but, in her memory, art and play stand for him and for the experience they shared that night.

In the car, she was conscious of the silence but couldn't think what to say to this man she hardly knew. At two o'clock on a Sunday morning, there was only sporadic traffic, but he had still driven slowly. The flattering thought, yes, she remembers thinking it was flattering that he might want to prolong the time spent in her company, yes, that excited her briefly but then it crossed her mind he was probably trying to avoid interest from the police. In the half an hour before they left, she saw him drink the best part of a bottle of wine and she could only imagine how much he had before. As they approached North Sheen, she realised that, within a minute or two, she would have to ask him to take a left and then, after a couple more turns, they would arrive at her street and the evening would be over. He would disappear from her life and she might never see him again. Never see him again. She felt the pain of anxiety at the thought.

When she looked back on that evening, she realised that what mattered most was the excitement she felt, the undefined desire, but not for the man himself, rather it was for the flutter in her chest that she remembered from her youth. She longed to resurrect the tremble in her inner being and perhaps the pain at the thought that she would never see this man again was nothing more than an unacknowledged longing to change her life. Not that she could have formulated it in so many words at the time. Such realisations always came later, sometimes too late. The years of her marriage and the years of her widowhood, up until that evening anyway, were calm. Her days passed in their uniformity, and she took whatever came her way as inevitable at her age. She took it for granted that she was invisible, as women over sixty are, with their grey hair and wrinkles, but that evening she felt, and she was surprised at the feeling, that she missed the flutter in her chest, the excitement at the possibility of being loved and loved in a way she craved, in a way that disturbs and unsettles. And with that realisation came self-reproach at being hopelessly romantic, sentimental even, in her mature age. Such a thought was unwarranted, she would say now, thirty years later, because she has realised that regardless of age, everyone needs love or, at least, everyone dreams of being loved. But when she considers that, the word yuck comes to mind and she admits to herself she would be ashamed to say the sentence about the need for love in front of anyone for fear of sounding as a heroine from a pulp fiction novel. No, she has never been a reader of such books and she mustn't think like one.

But that night in the car, she wondered whether she should invite the man who had used the word fuliginous in for a coffee to thank him for the lift. What if he misunderstood and laughed at her audacity, spurned her presumption? How she agonized. At sixty-two, she should have been beyond such concerns. In fact, she felt as socially gauche as she did as an adolescent. So much for age removing inhibition, she thought. She was as shy as she had always been. The only difference was that she was better at covering it up.

She remembers thinking, and thinking with relief, that at least she didn't have to worry about Martin; he was unlikely to be peering through his window on the off-chance there might be something interesting going on in front of her gate, two doors down the road. But what if he did catch a glimpse of her late-night visitor? What would he think of her?

What a ridiculous thought, she told herself, she remembers. More than ten years had passed since Bill died. She was entitled to a private life. It was none of Martin's business. He could hardly object if she offered a coffee to the person giving her a lift. After all, the man, Jon – or was it John? – was making sure she was safe; he has driven well out of his way, and it would only be polite to ask him in. She couldn't treat him like a taxi driver. Martin would agree, she remembers thinking. But, was it proper, she wondered, at this late hour, to encourage – encourage? The word made her pause, she remembers. Is that what it would be? – a man she had met only a few hours earlier? What would he take her for? Patricia would have known what to do; she was more than *au fait* with the etiquette of dealing with strangers in the early hours of the morning. But Patricia was in Scotland visiting her aged parent and, in any case, she couldn't be ringing her well past midnight to ask for advice. The car was about to turn into the street leading to hers and, in a few minutes, she will have to direct him where to stop. And when he did, should she wait for him to speak? She had already changed her mind five times. But what if he stopped the car but left the engine running as if expecting her to get out without any further ado? Or, even worse – would that be worse? – if he parked and turned the engine off? Would she have to invite him in then? Should she be affronted by his presumption? But once the seed had been planted in her mind, she could hardly remain silent. If he didn't, she would have to act. She remembers the confusion she felt at the thought: What seed? Excitement? Expectation? Seduction? The seed of seduction? Get real, Claire, what are you thinking about? You are sixty-two. Sixty-two but thinking like a teenager, and a silly one at that.

That party was Millie's idea. 'You must start socialising; it would do you good to meet new people. It's unhealthy to be alone all the time.' She could hear Millie's voice. But she wasn't alone. She saw Martin every day. Millie read her thoughts: 'Martin doesn't count. He's an odd sod, an old misanthrope. You will grow strange like him.'

Why shouldn't she carry on in the same way, if she was happy with her life? Besides, Martin was a most caring friend. But she knew better than to argue with Millie. It was going to be a long night, what with the concert before. She planned to make her excuses after the concert, say she had a headache and make her way home, but Millie and Max joined forces; they wouldn't hear of it.

'I can see you're getting cold feet. Come on, Claire, make an effort. You're too young to wait for death, shuffling around in your slippers. A party, that's what you need,' Millie said.

Typical Millie, she always knew what others needed. And unfair to boot. She had a busy life. She worked. She took regular walks with Martin and Poirot. She never missed a major exhibition, she saw lots of theatre, films. But there was no point arguing with Millie. Okay, it was true that she had dropped her reading group after more than three years but only because it was dominated by a boring man who imposed his choice of novels about grumpy old men fearing death, the characters forever banging on about prostate problems. And, she had attended two courses on French patisserie. She was hardly leading the life of a hermit, she remembers thinking. But to whom was she trying to justify her life? The truth was that she didn't need much persuading to accompany Millie and Max to the party. It was all a show, a show for the part of herself that was too shy to accept that sixty-two didn't mean the end of life. Why did she buy a new dress if she had no intention of going to the party? Not for the concert. She had enough clothes for such occasions. But this time, because of what was to follow the concert, she wanted to feel special, she wanted to feel confident, she wanted to feel different, she wanted to leave behind the years of marriage and the years of widowhood.

Sitting in the car, next to the man, whose profile – a strong, slightly hooked nose and a prominent chin – she had been admiring from the passenger seat for the past half hour, she was beginning to wonder whether Millie had a point about the importance of meeting other people. She remembers she sensed something mysterious about the man, something that intrigued her, something that made him unlike anyone else she had ever known. And then that same thought came to her mind that she might never see him again and she was gripped by a feeling of loss and she knew she needed to act and act urgently, say something, prolong the moment. She remembers she thought he liked her, at least enough to flirt. But what if he was one of those men who flirted with any woman and was only being kind in offering her a lift? Either way, she remembers, she couldn't trust her judgement.

She remembers that as soon as they had arrived, Millie and Max disappeared, and she was alone in a crowded room where she didn't know anyone. A few nervous approaches resulted in one-minute, stilted exchanges before the other person excused themselves and rushed off to whoever they 'had to talk to'. She felt lost. She hated the idea that she was lost because being lost was part of her previous life. The concert had been brilliant but the uncomfortable atmosphere at the party was ruining the memory of the elation she had felt watching the pianist's fingers in their dance across the keyboard. Why had she let herself be persuaded to go to the party? She didn't need anything else to make her evening. It was good to share a drink with Millie and Max during the interval but afterwards she felt like going home and curling up with a book. She remembers thinking that she should have been more assertive. She wanted to ring somebody, both to cheer herself up and to give the impression to everyone else in that crowded room that she was alone because she was busy making a call rather than because no one noticed her but then she realised that she had left her mobile in her jacket in the hall and couldn't face fighting her way through the chattering crowd to fetch it. She remembers, it was one of the first mobiles that were around. Bill had bought it for her after his heart attack so that he could reach her if needed. They were large, heavy objects, like bricks, bricks with a pair of aerials that needed to be extended for use. She probably wouldn't have been able to squeeze through the crowd anyway; to most of those people she was invisible, and they were unlikely to make way to allow her to pass.

Glass in hand, she wandered through the French doors into a garden lit by lanterns hidden in the bushes. She remembers that the air was saturated by the scent of trees in blossom but her urban nose failed the identification test. She was wearing high heels and after leaving the patio, she wobbled along the narrow-cobbled path that wound its way down the garden, as far as a stream that cascaded over a small waterfall. She sat down on a wooden bench, barely a yard from the edge of the stream; the party was a distant murmur, lost in the splashing of the water against the stones. She closed her eyes. It was relaxing; the water music allowed her to dream. She was somewhere else, not trapped by a group of loud people she didn't know. She felt light-headed; the image of the pianist's fingers made her dizzy with envy. If only she still had the ambition of youth, and the drive to practice, she remembers thinking. She was regretting growing old. Growing old! She wasn't growing old, she was old, she told herself. Old without realising that mysterious something, that something that is born from the joy and the pain of the urge to create, that something that makes you feel alive. How silly she was to think she was old, she thinks now. To think it was too late. But it is too late now.

She remembers she didn't hear anyone approach and had no idea how long he had been standing behind her. A voice said, 'would you like another drink?' and that, she remembers, brought her back from her reverie but it took her a second or two to realise that he was addressing her. She turned around and, against the lights from the house, she made out a gangly silhouette. Had he followed her into the garden, she wondered, she remembers.

'Are you expecting someone?' he asked.

'No,' she said quickly, having no idea what he meant. 'Why would I expect anyone?' Immediately, she regretted the hostile tone.

'A tryst in a dark corner of the garden.' His voice was serious, despite the irony. 'I saw you walk out with determination. I was sure you had an assignation, a secret assignation in the bushes.'

She remembers wondering whether he was being serious. 'I didn't realise it was that kind of party,' she said smiling, pleased with herself for being able to sound casual and project a level of self-confidence, even though a tryst was the last thing on her mind.

'Every party is that kind of party if you want it to be,' he said and waited for her to respond. When she didn't, he changed tack:

'Would you like a top up? Your glass is empty,' he said.

She declined: she had drunk too much already. He teased her for being puritanical. He wondered whether she wasn't enjoying the party and she struggled to respond in case he was the host or a close friend. He sat down next to her. He held a bottle in one hand and a glass in the other. He steadied the bottle on the ground between his feet.

'I don't blame you. This lot are terrible bores. They all have their freedom passes but their parties are no different from what they were forty years ago. Only the décor has changed, and they drink from expensive glasses instead of plastic cups. The conversation is as trivial and pompous as when they were students. They'll be putting on the Rolling Stones in a minute.'

He had a lot of baggage. She remembers asking him what he would prefer to talk about?

'I don't know. Things that matter. But not whose child has bagged which job and what they are buying their grandchildren for their next birthday.'

'You don't have any grandchildren?'

'God, no! You have to have children before you can have grandchildren and I've managed to avoid that particular predicament. I was a wise young man, even if I've turned into a foolish old one.' She remembers she wondered whether he was a genuine cynic or whether this was his party piece, something to wheel out with strangers.

She laughed.

'But you do disagree, don't you? You think grandchildren are sweet, or cute; isn't that the word they use?' Too shy to tell him what she thought, she shrugged. She remembered that moment later and thought how she had always played by the rules of small talk, always agreed in that anodyne, unconfrontational manner, always said what others wanted her to say. Bill had expected that from her.

'I bet you have a few. Cutie-cutie little ones,' he sneered. 'Here comes granny,' he chirped.

'No, I don't have any grandchildren.'

'One on the way then.' She couldn't see his face, but the mocking tone was clear.

'No. I don't have any children either.' She remembers thinking that it was the first time in her life that she could say it without feeling pain. And she liked him for that.

'To a fellow soul, a sensible soul,' he said and raised his glass.

She remembers every word they said. She remembers the sound of the water cascading against the stone feature. There was chill in the air and she wondered if Millie and Max were ready to leave. She turned towards the man and said she was going to get her jacket and look for the friends who had brought her. It was well past one o'clock. The man asked who her friends were and when she described them, he told her he had seen them leave half an hour earlier. He referred to them as crusty people. She was going to call a taxi but he said he too was leaving and would take her. She remembers saying that she didn't want to impose. Richmond was hardly on his way to Hampstead. He did not so much insist as assume they would leave together. In a matter-of-fact voice he said that it would be good to drive through West London at this time of night. She wondered what he meant but didn't ask.

'We're almost there,' she said.

She directed him to turn left but the road was blocked. They took the diversion and found themselves on Petersham Road.

'I used to love the view from here,' he said, his head gesturing towards the river bathed in moonshine. 'The way the river loops, just like a Constable painting.'

He seemed almost dreamy but then checked himself. He turned towards her and said with more emphasis than was needed: 'Not that I'm a fan of Constable.'

The real Constable view was from up the hill but before she could point that out to him, he added: 'And when I was young, they had cows grazing in that field.'

They still did but she couldn't see any at that time of the night. She said that she had often seen cows sitting down in the meadow by the river, yes, she distinctly remembers using the word meadow, and added that someone had told her that cows sitting down was a sign of rain on the way. She didn't know why she said that since she could see no cows, sitting or standing, except that something about the manner of the man she had known for barely an hour, something about the way he talked in that casual, over-confident way that both impressed and frightened her, made her utter words without considering them beforehand. She remembers thinking that he had an air of smugness. The way he took it for granted that she would accept his offer of a lift made her timid and self-conscious. To compensate, she talked too much, she talked for the sake of talking, for the sake of breaking the silence, and there was little chance she might say anything clever or remotely impressive. She remembers thinking that a woman of her age should not have to resort to trivial babble to cover up whatever it was, her shyness, her nervousness, or her lack of recent experience of the social discourse required when she found herself alone with the man she has met at a party, a man whom she might find intriguing, even if she couldn't tell in what way, a man not necessarily attractive in himself, but attractive as a proposition, as a novelty in her quiet, uneventful life. Those were the possible reasons why she mentioned the cows, and as soon as she did, she remembers that she knew her words would sound silly. Unlike many other people she can think of, people who would, in the presence of a stranger be gentle and kind, gentle and kind for the sake of kindness, gentle and kind for the sake of the weak, the underdog, the people who would attribute the silliness of the words of the other in their company to the potential awkwardness of the situation and say something about the idea being interesting even if it was an urban myth – or was it meant to be an old wife's tale? – and raise the question of how such beliefs came into existence, and the entire conversation would be forgotten with no consequence for anyone's confidence, with no judgements passed or implied by the interlocutor and no one would be made to feel uncomfortable, she knew immediately that wouldn't be the case with this man. He seemed to be well-versed in scoring points and, like a dog smelling fear, finding someone who was too weak to oppose him only encouraged him. She might have given the impression that she was in awe of him – no, she wasn't, she remembers she wasn't – and when she thought about it later, she knew that it was he who had been shy and lacking in self-assurance and that his over-confidence was bluster, acting, and poor acting at that, because he was not good at covering his shyness, despite being close to, or perhaps over, seventy years of age. But that was not something she thought at the time when, in accordance with his patronising manner, he smiled, and it was a supercilious smile, a smile that said yes, you are the kind of woman, yes, woman, he wouldn't have said a person, who believes in such things and I don't think I would have expected anything different from you. She doesn't remember the exact words that accompanied his smile, but their effect was to make her feel even sillier and it further undermined her confidence. She was ashamed of making herself appear credulous, or would it have even been superstitious? But she could have still saved herself had she had the presence of mind. She could have thought of something to say to make him pause and consider her words, even respond to them, rather than dismiss them and dismiss them in such a contemptible manner. She could have said something about the way irrational, old beliefs survive and how sometimes people use them to create a sense of certainty in an uncertain world. But she didn't have the presence of mind. Despite her feelings of inadequacy and shame, she carried on sitting next to this man in his car parked off the road leading west from Richmond Park at two o'clock on a Sunday morning without having the slightest inclination to leave his company or reach her home as quickly as possible, as you might expect the recipient of that supercilious smile to do. Moreover, she remembers she experienced a slight feeling of panic that she would soon be alone and most likely never see this man again, this man who was full of himself and who made her feel inadequate.

For a long time after that early Sunday morning she thought about her reaction to the situation at that point and concluded that, even though ten years had passed since the death of her husband, at sixty-two she was still thinking of herself as a child, a person watched over by a responsible adult. She had married in her early twenties, a man who had been more than two decades older than her and who spontaneously assumed the role of a parent to her, and not only because she was an orphan at twenty but also because her behaviour, the paralysis that she felt at the time, allowed, and possibly encouraged, involuntarily encouraged, Bill to act in loco parentis. After more than thirty years of marriage, she had become used to being looked after, used to having decisions made on her behalf and therefore, even without her husband being around, she remained passive and, perhaps even more importantly, she saw herself as passive. She remembers that was the image she had of herself, even though, once she was on her own, she managed the practical aspects of her life perfectly well, she made all the required decisions without hesitation or delay, as well as conducted her financial affairs, all those tasks that she used to think were exclusively the domain of an adult, her husband. Despite her ability to manage perfectly well on her own, she continued to think of herself as someone who needs looking after, someone who is passive, who doesn't make trouble, someone who lets events take their course. Throughout her adult life, Bill looked after her. He looked after her and she was grateful for that. That's what Bill thought. That's what everyone thought. That's what she thought. One day Patricia said she was like an object, carried on by the force of a stream that was Bill. An object unconscious of the current, not so much indifferent to where it was to end, but accepting whatever happened, slowly disintegrating until it disappeared. She dismissed those unkind words. But later, many years after his death, she looked back on her marriage and one day it occurred to her that the woman married to Bill had nothing to do with her. It was someone who had been impersonating a wife, the wife Bill needed.

The sense of passivity, or more correctly, the image of being an object with no will of her own became an inalienable part of the way she saw herself. She remembers that passivity and detachment became her default attitude to everything around her. In the car on the road leading west from Richmond Park, she was confused and scared, yes, scared too, but she waited. She waited because it was not in her nature to act. She waited for events to take their course. That was her default attitude. But she also remembers willing something to happen, something unexpected. She was anxious too, not because she thought the man next to her was a serial murderer, but she was apprehensive of making a fool of herself and, in a bizarre way, it was that apprehension, that entirely to be expected apprehension, which was exciting. When she looked back, she wondered if it was the challenge presented by a situation she had never experienced that was exciting and that, despite her fear, allowed her to enjoy the moment, an enjoyment of a kind that was new for her. Such contradictory feelings, feelings she wasn't aware of at the time, or rather, didn't have a chance to consider and acknowledge, brought about a sense of anticipation that something unusual was about to happen and the anticipation, she remembers, gripped her in a way that assuaged the shame of her silliness. She remembers that her instinct prevented her from confronting the man about his unkindness because she thought her intervention might have inhibited further development, which would have put an end to the situation, if he decided, as a result of her challenge, to drop her at home with a simple, curt good night. She sensed instinctively that he was the kind of man who needed a weak woman so that he could act. And she wanted him to act. Had she confronted him for being unkind, she might never have known what would have happened had she not intervened. But, of course, she was not conscious of such calculations. She felt excited about the what next. For she sensed that something was to happen. While it was not a situation of her choosing, there was a buzz around it, and the last thing she wanted was to put a stop to it. Thinking back, she couldn't even say that she didn't like the man as such thoughts didn't cross her mind. Had she had time to think about the situation, she might have realised that her amusement, if not bewilderment, was born from a sense, no matter how vague, that at her age, something unexpected, something she has never experienced, was about to happen and that she wanted it to.

She remembers he asked her whether she would like to take a walk and without waiting for her answer, he parked the car. They sat in silence and stared ahead. She racked her brain for something to say but, in front of him everything that came into her head seemed banal. The cows sitting down presaging rain. She wondered what was on his mind. After a few minutes, without saying a word, he turned towards her, his face expressionless. As if in slow motion, he placed his hand on her chest, just below the neckline. She remembers his cold, bony hand on her skin. The hand remained still, as if he was trying to assess whether she minded. Her heartbeat accelerated. She remembers that a lump appeared in her throat. He stroked her breasts through the dress, moving his hand very gently, barely touching the material. Her whole body tingled. She took a deep breath. Slowly, his hand moved underneath the neckline of the dress, slipped under her bra and cupped each breast in turn. She remembers that he held them as if measuring their weight. A moan escaped from her mouth.

Later, she remembers, she considered his audacity and wondered if she had unwittingly transmitted signals of her availability during the journey but she dismissed the thought. He was a man whose confidence was entirely internal, fed by his inflated sense of self-importance, bordering on arrogance. At the time, she was startled by the speed at which things happened, impressed by his dexterity in moving over the gear box with one elegant swoop of his body, and almost instantly releasing the handle that allowed him to push her seat back and create space for him to sit astride her, face to face. She remembers that he was considerate enough to keep his weight on his legs, which must have been quite a feat for someone of his age.

She remembers his kisses as deep and overpowering, like warm waves entering her mouth; they left her short of breath, but she didn't want them to stop. Not that he was giving any signs of tiring. She remembers thinking that he kissed her as if he had been starved of affection, as if she was the most desirable woman in the world. Then he was quick with the zip on the back of her dress and expert at releasing the hook of her bra, but he needed help removing her tights. She thought quickly: it was enough to bare one leg and slip the knickers over. She came almost as soon as he entered her, but his fingers continued sliding against her clitoris. She threw her head back, drunk with the excitement. She enveloped him tightly, her fingers sliding down his back. He moved inside her until she felt his body stiffen and he was spent. She remembers the feeling of joy. Bliss. She remembers. Like never before. She remembers.

As soon as she was breathing more steadily, she became aware of her surroundings. Had anyone been watching them? A policeman perhaps; they could be arrested for gross indecency. She remembers a headline flashed in front of her eyes: ageing piano teacher in car sex frolic. How bizarre to think that. But that was her in those days. She shouldn't have cared. The ageing piano teacher had just experienced her first orgasm with a man.

He didn't seem to be in any hurry to move and she remembers feeling grateful to him for holding her gently in his arms like no one had held her for many years. He planted kisses on her forehead.

'Your eyes are so blue, like a child's,' he said.

Yes, she thought. Yes.

❧

She remembers the morning after. She didn't wake up until the afternoon, the first time it had happened in many years, possibly the first time since her early twenties, and her first thought was: what would Bill have said? 'My dear, little Claire, what have you done? My dear, little Claire is again my lost, little girl.' Bill liked a quiet life and that meant routine, regularity. Anything unexpected, out of the ordinary, would upset the quietness of his life and he wasn't prepared to tolerate it. She went along with him most of the time without complaint, but even after he was dead, she stuck to the routine, sometimes consciously, sometimes unconsciously. She remembers thinking that it saved her, the routine saved her, she used to repeat it to herself when she didn't feel like doing something but believed it was necessary for her to keep going in the same way. But the morning after, she awoke past midday and that was out of the ordinary. That was a break with the routine. She didn't realise it at the time, but it was the first day of her new life, the new Claire. She did think what Bill would have said, yes, she remembers, how absurd that the first thing on her mind was what Bill would have thought of his dear, little Claire. But then, the anxiety she used to experience when she worried what he would say disappeared at a stroke and she laughed, yes, she laughed, she laughed loudly. She was Claire, but she wasn't anyone's Claire, let alone their dear, little Claire. She was Claire, a grown-up woman, for the first time at the age of sixty-two she was grown-up, her own woman with her own desires. She didn't have to answer to anyone but herself. She remembers she wasn't shocked at waking up so late and lazing about in bed. She remembers that what did surprise her was her nonchalant attitude that it was okay to do things differently, that it was fine to break away from the routine of her life, from the forty-year order. She was relaxed, and she remembers she stayed in bed, luxuriating in one of those moods where time stops and the mind dances with memories, memories resurfacing briefly, only to disappear and give way to other images, other smells, other voices from the past.

And today, it is not the morning after, hah, there are unlikely to be any more mornings after, but memories surge, fighting for attention, placing themselves one on top of the other, like hands in a child's game. She wants to hold onto them and re-live the palimpsest that is her life and she wants to remember everything. Memory is all. Memory is her life now. She must remember to call Zach and remind him to buy a box of macarons for Martin. But no, she knows there is no need. Zach would have remembered. The caring Zach. He always remembers everything she asks him. That's kind, that's what being caring means, not having to be reminded to do something for and by those one cares about. Zach has been buying the same birthday present for Martin for the past thirty years. It would be silly of her to remind him.

How interesting that Martin only likes green macarons, pistachio flavour and yet she has never told him about the green macarons in the Paris of her youth. Perhaps that's what they have in common, she and Martin. A special affinity for pistachio macarons. Perhaps he could have been her friend even if she had not married Bill. But it was Nick and his gift boxes from 'Le Macaron Rose' that developed Martin's taste. She will mention it to Gabriel. Is there a story in that? A story of coincidence. But coincidence for her, not for Martin, because he doesn't know about her green macarons in Paris. Isn't life full of coincidences? Sometimes it takes a long life, as long as hers, to spot them. One needs the perspective of time to see a pattern. But in the end, what does it mean? It's amusing. Nothing else.

She remembers once meeting a woman who told her that her

favourite poet, who had died in 1914, shared the date of death, and she told her the day, and the month, with a painter's model – was it Manet's model? – who had died in 1927, yes, Victorine Meurent, yes, the name comes to her now, and with the woman's grandfather in 1970. And the woman said that all three people were important in her life and she thought it meaningful that they shared their date of death. But what meaning? The woman didn't know but was sure there was something mysterious. And she remembers agreeing with her because she thought it was kind to humour her belief, the belief which, silly as it is, was making the woman happy. Why deprive her of that? A harmless illusion. Or is it? Is it a harmless illusion to think that there is a pattern, that there is meaning in what happens? It must work for some, for those with the temperament for religion, a need for belief. She didn't tell the woman that if she wanted to find meaning she would always find it. One always does. A figure in the carpet, as in the Henry James story.

Yes, Zach will be there with Gabriel and Gabriel will have a copy of his new book to give to Martin. A birthday present from one writer to another. A birthday present with a dedication, always the same dedication, 'In love and gratitude to Martin, a most admired colleague'. In gratitude, Gabriel always says, because Martin was the first person to believe in him. Did he? Or was it a way of getting closer to her? Was it a way of telling her, in those days when things were strained, I know Claire, you may not read my books anymore, but I have some clout with agents and publishers. Maybe that will get you to take notice of me. But his agent wouldn't have taken on Gabriel had she not seen earning potential, a healthy commission. They are business people. But it was kind of Martin. Kind to her, kind to Zach. And why not, he is fond of Zach. She remembers the three of them having dinners together in the time before Gabriel. The two of them cooking and then Zach arriving later, sitting in between them at the table. Like a proper family with a grown-up child, flanked by his parents. Years and years of those dinners, later with Gabriel too. The French have an expression, *une famille recomposée*. But they mean something different by that. But why not extend the meaning of the term? Yes, the three of them were *une vrai famille recomposée*. What if Bill could have seen them? That's a funny thought, a funny thought that had never crossed her mind until now.

When she was young she couldn't have imagined that someone a hundred and two would need a birthday present, or anything else for that matter. 'Reason not the need,' Lear says. Now she knows that at ninety-two she is more vulnerable to loneliness and she appreciates presents more than ever. They are the signs that someone cares for her and wishes to please her. Zach understands and indulges her.

Martin once asked how the two of them had met. She remembers they were standing in the kitchen, having just finished dinner and, on hearing the question, Zach turned away as if to fill the kettle, but she remained composed. But why shouldn't she have? There was nothing wrong with the way they met. People meet in music shops all the time. 'And then we talked for a good hour in a café,' she remembers telling Martin. 'Yes, Zach is an expert on jazz,' she remembers saying. Martin raised his eyebrows. But Zach was not a threat. Thirty-years her junior. Not a threat. That's what she thought. By then her Jocasta days were behind her. Now she has a son who is sixty-two. The age she was when she met Zach. Jocasta. Patricia laughed at that. Dear Patricia. She misses Patricia. Does she miss Bill? Years ago she would have felt guilty at the answer but not now. Guilt about the past, that's regret, which is pointless. She has finished with all that. As they say these days, she doesn't do guilt.

Not consciously. As for that dream, she can't control what comes when she is asleep. She has a different life now. She was happy with Bill, or so she thought, but she is very happy now. He wouldn't begrudge her. He loved her. In his own way.

Dear Zach. He calls her Claire. That pleases her. She likes the way he says her name, prolonging the middle, enjoying the sound. She hears love in his voice. He called her that from the beginning. She remembers she used to think that if she had children, she would like them to call her by her first name, certainly once they were no longer babies. In public, she is his mother. Not a stupid assumption to make. She remembers Patricia meeting him. Meeting him afterwards, yes after she stopped playing the role of Jocasta. She remembers the two of them sitting in the members' room at the Royal Academy, with Patricia tucking into a large slice of a chocolate cake. That was predictable with Patricia, she could never resist. And the little performance, the little speech that she wasn't going to have it because they make them too sugary and it wasn't good for her health and at her age she had to be careful and in any case, she was always trying to lose weight and then once the monologue had finished, without fail, she would order the cake. She loved seeing Patricia do that. What the hell. One lives only once, she would say. And she was right. Dearest Patricia. Zach joined them in the cafe after the two of them had seen an exhibition. They got on straight away. Later, Patricia told her to try again. Try again? Was she joking? No, of course not. She said he was hot. Or was it cool? One of those stupid words Patricia liked to use, but use ironically, as if to show they were not her words, only borrowed. But she meant it. Patricia was silly then and she told her that. 'Everyone is bisexual,' Patricia said, 'whether they know it or not.' Not everyone. Many are, she remembers thinking, but not everyone. Not Zach. Definitely not Zach. Patricia shook her head. 'The right man or the right woman never came along.' You could always put it like that, she remembers thinking. But the right man came along for Zach. Gabriel. Dear Gabriel. His archangel.

Now they sit on Patricia's bench, the bench overlooking the river, with Marble Hill House behind them, Zach and her, sometimes Gabriel too. He knew her only briefly. It was another five years before he joined the family. The family? Yes, why not. *La famille recomposée*, and he is the son-in-law. She has said that more than once. The first time, she remembers, someone at a book launch, his book launch, asked her whether she was his reader. 'Yes,' she said, 'but I am also his mother-in-law.' And they said, something like, 'oh, you must be very proud', and she was. When they sit on the bench, she never fails to remember Patricia's anxiety about death, how she maniacally read dates engraved on the plaques on the commemorative benches. She did her calculations. Whenever the person had died younger than she was at the time, she panicked. She was living on borrowed time, she used to say. Does anyone do that with her dates now? A popular spot for memorials. The council said she was the last one to be given permission. It wouldn't have been so good anywhere else. That's where they walked. That's where Patricia checked the dates. Sixty-eight years, that's all she got. On the positive side, it was quick. But how can it be positive since Patricia didn't know it? Positive for those who stayed on. Stayed on? It's not a party. No, but she can't complain. At least it was quick. When Millie heard, she said, 'I want to go like that.' We all do, don't we? But Millie didn't 'go like that'. Millie spent five years not recognising anyone, deaf and partially blind, incontinent, shouting nonsense in several languages. She had to be tranquillised. Tranquillised? Is that the right word? That's for animals, isn't it? But what they do and why they do it is the same. Yes, the word comes to her now. Sedated. Yes, Millie was sedated. Max looked after her together with two carers. He died before her. Millie carried on, unaware. She wondered, what was worse? Being conscious of one's deterioration or not? Probably being conscious.

Knowing what is going on. A small mercy for Millie, then. With Millie, it was the heart that kept ticking on. Her big heart. She could be fierce, but she had a big heart. Millie was open, loud and generous. So straightforward that it could hurt. It hurt those who didn't know Millie. Not her. She never minded Millie's bluntness. And Millie couldn't mind about her dying, a five-year dying. She had no mind to mind. Gosh, let it go Claire, why is language chasing you now? Making her play silly word games.

She remembers a funeral where a relative of the deceased told her about her two aunts. One was still nimble on her feet but unaware of the world, did not know who she or anyone else was. She zigzagged around the mourners, smiling at people and her son had to pull her back, as if she were a toddler who had just learned to walk. The other was *compos mentis* but immobile and couldn't attend. A double act in a farce. Which had the worse deal? A silly question. One can't choose. Except if you take the matter into your own hands. Like that friend of hers. That architect. But they are known to be the profession fifth most likely to do it. She has forgotten who was the first. Writers? Artists?

She remembers ringing the daughter. They were meeting at the Tate and Patricia hadn't turned up. No answer from her mobile. She knew something was wrong. Martin said she always thought the worst. But this time she was right. She imagined Patricia lying on her back on the floor in the entrance hall of her house. The daughter only went over the next day; she had a builder at home or something like that. She took her own daughter, a twelve-year-old girl, not fazed at all, the mother said, seeing Patricia lying on her back in the hall. Exactly as she had imagined. The girl covered her granny with a sheet, the daughter said. Aneurysm. But was it brain or heart? She was never told although she did ask, she remembers, several times. But what does it matter?

The dream. The first time it came to her was after she had met Jon in Richmond Park. The day after their tryst in Richmond Park. Would he have thought of it as a tryst? Would he have spared a thought for her afterwards? She couldn't tell. She remembers that she didn't know what to call their dalliance. Dalliance? That's a silly word. A one-night stand until then. That was clear. But afterwards? A two-night stand?

It was the brain with Bill, or that's what she thinks because Bill used to say he thought he might have an aneurysm, but the coroner reported an accidental death. Death as an accident. An accident as death. She didn't know which aneurysm Bill had. Or thought he had. She told them what she knew. But the police asked again and again. No, she didn't notice anything unusual. She prepared dinner, she told them. They asked what was on the menu. A strange word, she thought. There was no menu. She wasn't running a restaurant. She chose what they ate. But she didn't say that. In any case, it wasn't her cooking that killed him. But she didn't say that either. In these situations, it's best to stick to the point and answer the question. It was pasta, one of his favourite dishes. Pasta with mushrooms. They wanted to know which type of mushrooms. Organic, chestnut, button mushrooms, nothing exotic or unusual, she told them. And there was a sauce. She didn't wait for them to ask. Italian, from a jar. 'Was it a truffle sauce?' the woman asked. Her favourite, the woman said. That was hardly relevant but perhaps she was trying to be nice. Or friendly. Win over her trust. Perhaps that's what they are trained to do and then the suspect . . . suspect? Was she a suspect? Later she wondered what the police had thought. It couldn't have been the first time they were in a situation like that. She showed them the jar. Always stocking up food, that was her habit, buying several of those truffle jars at the same time; she had one left. They took it away. Martin said it was for analysis. Martin, the detective novelist, turned adviser. Was she a suspect? Bill was seventy-five, a year after his stroke. Not a great age but death was hardly unexpected. No, Martin said, she wasn't a suspect, but the police routinely look into cases where a person is found dead at home. Bill was found dead. The ambulance arrived quickly, within minutes but they said he had been dead for an hour. That's why they called the police. A normal procedure. It was an early dinner, she told them. They were sitting in the lounge sipping tea, going through the list of things they still needed to do before flying to New York the next day. It was her delayed birthday present. They couldn't have gone for her fiftieth – Bill always liked to celebrate landmark birthdays with something different, 'something special' – because he had a kidney infection. A few days after he had recovered, he collapsed with a stroke. But he was fine, recovered by that evening. So they waited another year before booking. By that time she was almost fifty two. And so after dinner, on the eve of flying to New York, she went to the kitchen to switch on the dishwasher. It was still full that morning, she told the police, they could go and check. Why did she say that? Was she worried? No, but her adolescent shyness, her lack of confidence, still prevailed. Not now. In those days she used to be like those people who blush when something is stolen, those people who blush even though they had nothing to do with the theft, and people take their blushing for guilt. While she was out of the room, in the kitchen, doing the dishwasher, the phone rang. She knew it was Patricia and she decided to take it in her music room, the room with the piano, she told them. 'Do you remember what time the call came,' the male officer asked. 'Not exactly,' she remembers saying; it was easy to check. Well, they should know that. Telephone records. That was her saying too much again. Would her chattiness have made them more suspicious? They asked which way she walked from the kitchen to the music room. Through the hall and past the double glass door. Yes, she did see something, she caught a glance of Bill no longer sitting up. He was lying down but lying on the sofa. There was nothing unusual about it. No, he wasn't on the floor. Definitely not. Yes, she would have checked him, she wouldn't have walked past him to her room had he been lying on the floor. But why didn't she take the call in the lounge? Because Bill was not too fond of Patricia and she knew it would not be a short call. Sometimes he would be irritated by her friend. Well, always, but she didn't say that. 'We talked for a long time, an hour,' she said. What did they talk about? Was that relevant, she remembers thinking. Why did they want all these details when they had already told her that it was only a formality? Only a short report. She did answer that. She had to, in case they checked with Patricia. Patricia wouldn't have minded. She was always open about the nitty gritty of her dating. When the call ended, Bill was still lying in the same position, occupying the length of the sofa. She sat in the armchair next to the sofa and was about to tell him that he should go to bed, when she noticed that there was an unusual grimace on his face; his mouth and his eyes were half open, his lips seemed rigid and distorted. Panic. She said his name, shook him. She tried to sit him up. She even slapped him. She knew that's what they do when someone has fainted. He was unconscious. Well, he was dead but dead is unconscious. Was that really happening, she remembers thinking. She called an ambulance. Yes, they asked whether he had fallen on the floor. They could tell he had been moved while dead. No, she didn't go with them. They didn't want her to. There was no point. She did as she was told. Stayed behind. When they drove off, they didn't switch on the lights or the siren. There was no point. And they told her that the police would come to speak to her. She remembers thinking they would come the next day, not straight away. And that's what happened. But she stayed waiting. She was still the Claire who obeyed. The next day when they came, first thing in the morning, she was even more confused. She hadn't slept. The woman said she could stay with her for support. No, she didn't need them. She had support. Her next door neighbour. They assumed it was a woman. She left it at that. What did it matter whether Martin was a Martina? She remembers thinking that. Who knows what assumptions they might have made. With all their suspicions about Bill's death, would they think she had a lover next door?

❧

Bill was forthright about Patricia. 'Too loud,' she remembers him saying. Obsessed with sex. She used to shrug. Why should she have to justify her friend to Bill? She thought he was jealous, and he probably was. But Martin? She could never tell why he didn't like Patricia. The feeling was mutual. 'That old fart,' Patricia called him. And Martin assuming a role as if he were an actor on the stage, or a character in a story. Whenever he saw Patricia, he became prickly and awkward. Was that his way of dealing with his feelings? Could he have secretly been interested in her? Bill said that was impossible. 'No one could be interested in Patricia.' She thought how unfair Bill was. And Martin. Silly men. Probably threatened by a strong woman. Yes, that's plausible. How had it never occurred to her before? Patricia was a strong, independent woman.

She remembers them walking together, Patricia working out the dates on the benches, as usual, agonizing that she was living on borrowed time as if the inscribed dates were some kind of norm, the norm applicable to her at least, when they spotted him, or Patricia did. In fact, it was Poirot she saw first. The dog running towards them.

'We can't really escape, can we?' Patricia asked while the dog snuggled up to her knees and waved its tail frantically.

'It'll be okay. Stay calm and let me do the talking,' she said.

'Calm? Me? You should know better than that.' Patricia had a sense of humour and self-knowledge.

Self-knowledge. The first time she heard about it was from Mr Gintz. How she remembers when certain words and ideas became known to her. Her old tutor of music history at Oxford, telling the class that not knowing oneself is the greatest sin in life and it was the problem faced by Shakespeare's tragic heroes, the reason why they all come to a sticky end. He told them that Renaissance culture placed great faith in *nosce te ipsum*, the need to know thyself, and that young people like them could do worse than adopt the same motto. He said it in almost every other lecture and then he would pause and look at the class with an even more serious expression than usual. She remembers he was a refugee from Austria, who spoke a dozen languages. His English was heavily accented and that, coupled with his tendency to quote Shakespeare at every opportunity, made him a constant target for mockery. *Nosce te ipsum*, delivered with a wagging index finger and a giggle, could be heard up and down the corridor. More than once, she witnessed a performance when the man himself was passing by and she felt embarrassed, worrying that he might feel hurt. But Mr Gintz had too much dignity to respond. Or perhaps he was simply engrossed in his own world and genuinely oblivious to the babbling of youth. She was one of the few students who had a soft spot for him. She took his advice, trying to be as self-reflective and aware of her limitations and desires. But then other things happened, and she forgot his counsel. Does she know herself now, does she know herself at ninety-two? Or is she still a sinner? Years after leaving university, she heard that Mr Gintz had taken early retirement and had died within a year. They said he had developed an obsessive-compulsive disorder. How strange to remember him now. He would spend hours trying to lock the door of his digs, repeatedly returning and checking the lock. She remembers someone telling her that Mr Gintz was a survivor.

But Patricia knew herself well enough. Her misfortune was that she didn't understand others, men in particular. She was so keen to have a relationship that she hardly noticed what they were really like. But isn't that true of her as well? Of most women, come to think of it. But that time, that time when they were surprised by Martin, she remembers him saying, 'Hello, ladies,' bowing histrionically and raising his hat. 'A repose on a bench after a constitutional perambulation. Taking air is good for your skin, they say.'

Even without looking at her, she knew Patricia was rolling her eyes. She remembers being grateful that Patricia didn't respond, which wasn't always the case in the face of Martin's assaults on the thesaurus. He bent down to pat Poirot. She remembers that. Those years with Poirot, so clever and emotional. Rare for a man, perhaps not so rare for a dog, she thought but that's not kind. Maybe it was true in those days. Not now. Zach and Gabriel are clever and emotional. Strong and affectionate. Real men. Her son and his partner. She will mention Poirot to Martin today. A little reminisce will do him good. What else can one do on a one hundredth and second birthday but reminisce?

'Good boy, you found these lovely ladies. And I can see you would like us to join them.' She can still hear Martin, as if it had happened yesterday. At ninety-two, everything is yesterday. Near and far away at the same time. But no, she mustn't get sentimental. Sentimentality is kitsch. She said that to Bill once and he looked at her as if she had spoken in Chinese. He said she didn't know what she was talking about. She didn't argue. But she was right. Sentimentality is kitsch.

And then, yes, after Martin suggested that Poirot wanted to join the lovely ladies, Patricia winced but moved to the side to make space on the bench.

'That's very kind of you but we shall have to decline your hospitality on this occasion,' Martin said. 'So, old boy, although the company of these ladies is enticing, we cannot stay.' She remembers his smile as he recited. And the pleasure in his voice. Martin the actor, a bad actor in front of Patricia.

'Where are you off to?' she asked. Martin never went anywhere. She was sure he was making an excuse.

'The annual MOT.'

That couldn't be true. He had it done a month earlier. She remembered picking him up from the garage.

'The annual health check-up,' Martin said. Another smile of satisfaction.

'You?' she asked.

'No, not me. I'm in the peak of condition, wet nose and wagging tail. It's the old boy. Poirot has an appointment with his veterinary consultant. So, ladies, I apologise but we have to take our leave. Duty calls.' He saluted again, and off they went, Poirot running ahead.

'Phew, that was lucky. Good boy Poirot. I should buy him a bone,' Patricia said. She was fanning her face with a newspaper and taking deep breaths. Patricia, always so confident, and yet so easily ruffled by Martin.

She remembers doubting that there was an appointment. He would have invented anything to avoid 'that loud friend of yours', his usual complaint about Patricia. How strange, from him who never complained about anyone. Not even after the rupture did he complain about Bill. And that happened suddenly, out of the blue. Utter joy, happiness and then cold. Hatred and silence from both. It was hard for her to navigate. She remembers the evening before the break, even Bill was relaxed, unusually relaxed. They laughed a lot. Martin had taken them to their favourite restaurant to 'celebrate the publication of my latest novel with my best friends'. She remembers Bill talking about his invitation to a conference in Japan, and for once, not worrying about the research he was presenting. She and Martin compared notes on recent exhibitions. No one mentioned Martin's book. It was just another detective novel. Bill read them from time to time but found it difficult to keep up with his friend's prolific output. She had stopped reading them years earlier. They were not the type of fiction she liked and Martin was too good a friend for her to have to pretend. After dinner, they walked home and had a nightcap in Martin's house. They had never laughed so much before. Life was beautiful. She remembers looking at Bill and thinking how lucky she was. That evening of happiness, of easy friendship, everyone relaxed, better than ever and then the end, sudden and brutal. She remembers lying in bed that night, full of the evening, and feeling jealous of Bill having such a good and long-standing friend. But perhaps she wasn't being fair. There was Patricia, she had Patricia, but they met later in life and, at the time, she didn't know that they would remain friends for life. When she mentioned Martin to Bill, he said they had clicked straight away: 'it happened over squash. Our respective partners didn't turn up for the arranged session and we both found ourselves alone. We played and the rest, as they say, is history.' A forty plus year old history. And she remembers Bill saying that now Martin was her friend too. Of course, and she had Patricia, too. As for Martin, in many ways, she had much more in common with him than with Bill. Besides, neither Bill nor Martin played squash anymore and, given their different career paths, they rarely did anything together, just the two of them. They had been next door neighbours for thirty years and all their socialising had involved her. But that wasn't the point. Martin became her friend only by extension, by marriage, as one acquires in-laws, whether one wants to or not. But with Bill and Martin, it was one of those friendships that endured the ravages of time and that didn't seem to require nurturing. They could take each other for granted. Or so she thought.

Many years ago she remembers reading somewhere that there are no real friends. There are only moments of friendship. A long moment it was for Bill and Martin. And for her and Patricia. Others have come and gone, but Patricia was a friend for life. Dead for twenty years now. Bill was jealous of Patricia. He used to say he could never have lived with anyone like Patricia. No, she wouldn't have been his 'dear, little'. Patricia was her own woman. No one's, dear, let alone little. She was too strong for him, and for most men it seems. Too strong for most men because most men lack self-confidence. Is that why Martin didn't like her? It couldn't have been Patricia talking about her sex life since she never talked to him about it. Was Martin asexual? What does it mean to be asexual? The right woman, or man, never came along? That's what Patricia would have said. In his novels, there was a lot of sex, pages of detailed descriptions. Not badly written either, she thought. They wouldn't qualify for the bad sex award. But how could he write so vividly, so convincingly, when during all the years she has known him, a lifetime really, there had never been anyone. She asked Bill once. Bill laughed and said it was all imagination. Or perhaps, wishful thinking, he added. But once, later, without her asking anything, he said Martin had been engaged and then the woman broke it off. She had been diagnosed with terminal cancer and she wanted to free him from his commitment. When she died, Martin was bereft. He was twenty-eight, the woman a couple of years older. 'Paradoxically, rather than freeing him, she seems to have tied him to her forever,' she remembers Bill saying.

She remembers the afternoon, the day after the celebratory dinner. It was pouring down as if in a dystopian novel where the rain never abates. Nature weeping for a friendship about to be destroyed. She remembers thinking how that afternoon she couldn't imagine any other weather but clouds and rain. She had been to a lecture at a gallery and had returned home earlier than planned. She had opened the door and Poirot ran to her from the lounge. He had seemed subdued and had started rubbing himself against her legs. She could tell something was wrong. She stroked him, talked to him and could hear his low whining. Then she heard shouting from the kitchen. The door was closed, and she sat down in the lounge, unwilling to interrupt, the dog quietly pressed against her. He had sensed something was out of place and soon she did too. She could hear Bill saying that he won't accept it. The book had to be withdrawn immediately. Martin claimed he was being silly to confuse fiction with real life. Dr Williamson was not Bill. Yes, there were some similarities, but one could always find resemblances with any fictional character. 'Look,' Martin said, 'my character lives with a young woman, he is not married. Yes, he uses prostitutes but so do lots of men.' 'Should I be grateful for that?' Bill shouted. He said that Martin had done it deliberately. 'You have, haven't you?' Bill said. Martin's response was that it was about time for some honesty with those 'close to you' and he stressed that Bill should know what he meant by that. Bill said he was asking for the final time whether Martin was prepared to withdraw the book. Martin offered to insert a note that any similarities with living persons were entirely coincidental and unintentional. At that point, Bill asked Martin to leave and never come back. Martin pleaded with him, but Bill opened the door. 'Anyway, she doesn't read your novels. Why should I worry?' she heard Bill say.

And then the sound of Martin's steps in the hall and the front door closed behind him. The next time he entered the house was after Bill's death, two years later. Bill never mentioned Martin after that afternoon. She could tell he was hurt. So was Martin. She didn't prod. Bill wouldn't have wanted to talk about it, so she didn't ask. Nor was she interested in the reasons. They both had their reasons. Bill always had his reasons. They were good reasons, she always told herself. She trusted his reasons even if she didn't know what they were. But perhaps she shouldn't have. Bill couldn't see other people's reasons. It was always only his position. Patricia noticed the same. But what did it matter? He was good to her and she loved him.

A long moment of friendship it was, half a century for Bill and Martin. But friends come and go. Not her and Patricia. Theirs was 'till death us do part'. Forty odd years. Their friendship was constant, and Patricia was constant with her lack of luck in love. She can see herself now, married for a couple of years, wandering in East London, looking for a piano tuner's shop. She was lost and asked the first person she saw for directions. 'I'm going the same way,' Patricia said, all chatty and friendly, open, very open, telling her about the stamina of her new lover and she listened, shy but fascinated. She had never heard anyone talk about sex so directly, let alone to a stranger. Patricia insisted on showing her a picture in a gallery they passed on the way. It was closed, it would have been a Monday, but she could see someone inside and kept banging on the door until they opened so that she 'could introduce my friend to a picture I love'. Patricia was more unconventional than anyone she had known. Before they parted, they exchanged phone numbers. 'I could tell what kind of person you were straight away,' Patricia told her later. But she didn't seem to be a good judge of her lovers.

A couple of days after they had met, she rang, in tears. The lover with 'incredible stamina' was two-timing. 'What a bastard, can you imagine, Claire, and he wanted to move in with me. Bastard,' she was shouting on the phone. There were many more bastards to come and go. It was always the same story. She died never finding a true love. But she never lost faith that it was possible.

❧

And how hard Patricia had worked on her to persuade her to join a dating agency. Her take was that everyone deserved to have fun and particularly women in their sixties. Why women in their sixties? 'Think of it like this,' Patricia said, 'the body is still okay, that's unless you have been unlucky, or careless. You have not been unlucky, unlucky to fall ill, or been careless, careless with a bad diet and too much drinking. And then there is no longer the fear of unwanted pregnancy, career and children are out of the way, so you can focus solely on pleasure.' The last could be true for many, she used to think, but not for the unwillingly childless ones. Children were not out of the way. Neither out nor on the way. How strange that Patricia never feared pregnancy. Dating, blind dating, wasn't her thing. Besides, she had needed those years alone, those years before that encounter with Jon. She had needed to grow up. To begin to grow up at fifty-one. And she had needed to see clearly. But did she really see clearly? Does she see clearly now? Isn't life always plodding on in the mud, in the murky waters of ignorance? But no, dating, blind dating was never for her. That much she knew. A few telephone conversations and a couple of blind dates, all of that was terrifying. But why? What was she afraid of? Many things. To start with, she remembers she was afraid of catching something. How embarrassed she was that time in the walk-in clinic. All those young people around, mostly in couples and she, an older woman, an older woman in her early sixties. It was after Jon. What was she thinking? She trusted him when he said he was okay. But that was later. Not the first time. She wasn't thinking anything the first time. Except of the cows and the full moon. Fuliginous sky. That word has stuck with her. She wasn't thinking of anything. Her body took over. Stopped her thinking. But he was right. There was nothing for her to be worried about. At one point it didn't look like that and she was convinced she had, what was it, genital warts? Yes, she looked in the mirror and was sure she had it. She remembers ringing Patricia to come with her, but Patricia was in Scotland, on one of her emergency visits to her dying mother. Patricia was kind. Be an adult about it. Nothing to be ashamed of. But she was. Terribly ashamed. A granny in the waiting room of a vd clinic. But she was okay. A false alarm. And later, always a condom. But she was still afraid, afraid of not being liked, not being liked by her blind date. She could see the men were nervous too, afraid of not being liked. But most tried to disguise it. And all the preparation, the make-up and clothes when you go on the blind date. How she hated all that. Maybe the man will disappear with an excuse to go to the toilet and never come back. Patricia said it didn't worry her. But then it happened and she was left with a large bill. That would have been particularly unkind. Taking off without settling his part. How she hates unkindness. Unkindness of any type. But at least Patricia got rid of the nasty person without further ado. 'Best if they show their true colours straight away,' Patricia said. If she could have a blind date now, would she still be afraid? Of course. Don't be silly, Claire. Who is going to meet a woman of ninety-two? He would have to be not only blind but mad too.

Where's that builder now? Would she still be as snobbish as she was then if he were to ring now and brag about his prowess?

No, blind dates were never her thing. But it must work for some people. Patricia blamed her Catholic upbringing, 'all that shame and guilt', but no, she had left that behind ages ago. What bothered her was the marketing aspect, the idea of 'selling yourself', like perishable goods. Perhaps she was an old romantic. Perhaps she would never have known Zach had they met through a dating agency. A music bookshop, looking at the same coffee table book of jazz photographs, that was much more romantic. There was nothing wrong with talking to a stranger there. And yet she didn't tell Patricia at the time. Was Patricia hurt? Perhaps a tiny bit, but she would have understood.

Isn't Gabriel's new book about people not talking to each other, even to those meant to be close to them? She is looking forward to reading the finished version. She is always the first to be given a copy; she has been acknowledged in all of them and she reads them. Of course, she does. She loves them. He is her kind of writer. Unlike Martin. With a good light and her reading glasses, she can still manage. All those green-leaf dinners must have paid off. She was lucky; she hadn't needed her reading glasses until she was sixty-five. Most people need them in their fifties. All those greens to slow down her macular degeneration. The greens. She remembers planting greens in the quad. No room for flowers. Vegetables all around the college. Women mostly. Women taking over Oxford. There were few men around immediately after the war. They were digging for victory. Well, not quite. The victory was there but the sentiment continued. In Oxford. It was lucky they had not been bombed. She had no idea of gardening. She remembers a few others, women from posh families, servants and all, and there in the College scrubbing floors, scrubbing floors for the first time. Joint effort. They didn't mind. She played her music and then went out planting, digging, weeding. They ate her greens. And she carried on eating greens all her life.

In Gabriel's latest novel, a couple in their eighties are walking through Richmond Park and reminiscing about their lives. They remember the picnics they had in the Park with their children and look back on their various summer holidays as a family, but their accounts of the same events are entirely disparate, and they argue, each claiming the truth of their version. They also touch upon politics and philosophy and again violently disagree. By the end of the walk, they hate each other, and each thinks it is best if they separate. It is the kind of novel that people, including critics, either love or hate as not much happens in the traditional sense. The characters simply walk and talk. It is her kind of novel. Is it Martin's? He wouldn't say it if it weren't. She will go to the book launch for the new one. She loves the occasions. Martin doesn't come anymore. 'Difficult to hear anything with the cacophony of voices,' he said. His hearing aids cannot cope with the party murmur.

Richmond Park. She and Bill used to drive through but rarely stopped for a walk there. Their walks were further afield. The Loire valley. Or the Dordogne. Périgord. Once she knew a young woman who was writing a PhD on Bertran de Born. A good musician she was, her student for many years. Talented and hard working. And beautiful to boot. Many years ago she heard her on the radio, an academic, expert on the troubadours. Was it a programme about troubadours, or was it about Périgord? She would be in her seventies now. Ursula. Yes, she was called Ursula. She remembers the first time the young woman came to her and said her name. She thought of D H Lawrence and *Women in Love*. Coloured stockings. That's what came to mind when Ursula, her new student, introduced herself. And Ursula, the surname escapes her now, some bird it was, she had written a book, lots of books, all on troubadours.

❧

That novel with the ageing couple is called *Richmond Park*. The second time with Jon was in Richmond Park. She remembers the casual tone of his phone message. As if he couldn't care less. He was to be in the area to see his dentist. 'Richmond Park for a walk?' he asked. She remembers thinking Richmond Park in the afternoon was not Petersham Road at two o'clock in the morning but still she wondered. The thought was exciting but then what was he taking her for? An easy lay? Her prudish self, her lapsed Catholic self, reared its head. No, she was not going to allow that. She would take her Wellingtons, make sure that he knew it really would be a walk. Martin saw her taking her boots to the car. Where was she going? He could join her, take Poirot for a walk. He had just finished a chapter and was taking the afternoon off. Oh no, she was meeting someone, a friend. He said he thought Patricia was in Scotland. No, this was someone she had met at her patisserie course. Not that Nick who was after her? No, it wasn't the tutor and, in any case, he wasn't after her. Martin disagreed, mentioned Nick always ringing with tickets for this and that. Of course, he was after her. She felt flustered. She told him she had to go. She left him sulking. She remembers thinking how they would need to have a chat. Yes, he had been a friend in need when she was widowed, always kind to her, always there for her, but she had the right to live her own life. Patricia had warned her to watch out. Martin was after her, she told her repeatedly. But she laughed it off. Patricia didn't like him. But perhaps she had a point. Putting his arm around her when they watched a film in her house a couple of times a week, no, she didn't want that. And those slippers he kept in her house. But how could she have refused? It was convenient but wouldn't have been such a big deal to bring them each time, well, every day in fact, since he was only next door. 'So, I don't have to remember to carry them over.' He did ask if she minded. He didn't take her for granted. But while she understood the symbolism, and possible danger, she thought she could indulge him, allow him the convenience for the sake of friendship. Keeping a pair of slippers in her house was no big deal, she remembers thinking but perhaps she was wrong. It was a big deal for him. A step on the way to . . . what? Moving in? Perhaps. After she had gone to Richmond Park without him, he sulked for days but they still remained friends. Not like with Nick.

That afternoon in Richmond Park, Jon was waiting for her by his car and they set out on a walk. The clouds were gathering and she worried about being caught in a storm. What if there was lightening, with all those high trees around? Should she lie on the ground, flat on the ground? Or was it, crouch, hold your knees? Bill would have known, she remembers thinking. Again, she was intrigued by Jon's ironic tone. He told her he was a GP but glad to be out of it. She remembers his laughter, his reaction when she asked whether he missed medicine: 'Oh, God, no! I was pretty fed up with it all by the end. I tried to take the grown-up line, tell them the truth, treat them like proper adults. But they didn't want that; they just wanted comfort and cures and, if I couldn't give them that, hope. They expect you to be a god, so in the end I started to behave like one and hated myself for it. But really, it's all witchcraft anyway. People usually get better on their own and, if they don't, you send them on to a higher deity. I would have been more usefully trained as an actor.' What a speech, she remembers thinking. He sounded as if he had played the part before and she had to agree, silently, that he would have been better at being an actor. Where is he now? He was Martin's age. Just possibly still alive. Possible but not likely. He was slim and fit, but that's not enough. Luck. It's all luck. She remembers him as an interesting cynic, a refreshing, amusing voice. It didn't occur to her then, but these days she wonders whether that's the only realistic position to take. Or is she too becoming cynical, a cynic at ninety-two? She remembers asking him what he was doing in retirement. He said he was a painter and he was holding an exhibition at a small gallery in Brixton but he had no illusions about art. When she told him he must be good to be able to exhibit, he said: 'Not at all. I only do it because painting's cheaper than gambling, not to mention safer. You have to mark the time somehow. I can't play the piano, not anymore. I did all the grades to please my mother but I was useless. Now that she's gone, I can do what I like.'

Drops of rain created wet circles on their jackets, but he didn't seem concerned. She remembers he teased her when she suggested turning back. It was too late to turn back anyway. But he had a solution. Maybe he planned it all along, she remembers thinking. A hut, a garden shed really. How strange it was there, in the Park.

She had never seen it before. And why does this thought come to her now, after all these years? He said they should take cover and bundled her in. She shivered. Was it nerves, or expectation? She remembers him asking if she was cold and then wrapping her in his heavy, waxed jacket, his arms tight around her. The rain was pounding the corrugated metal roof. A memory of their first meeting came to her. That time they listened to a different water music. She remembers him telling her not to worry. It wouldn't last long. A flash of lightening illuminated the inside of the shed and a couple of seconds later, thunder roared. He tightened his embrace. When the roll of thunder abated, he held her face between his hands and kissed her on the forehead. She remembers feeling like a schoolgirl caressed by a parent. Why did she stand so perfectly still? Why did she show more compliance than she would have liked? The obedient Claire of those days. He stepped back, his hands still holding her head and looked into her eyes as if trying to guess her thoughts.

'You're beautiful,' he said. The tenderness of the words surprised her. Never would she had expected compliments to be part of his vocabulary. She remembers thinking about it later and reminding herself that Jon was an actor *manqué*, there was nothing about him but the role. But isn't a role one plays all we can know about anyone? Didn't she too play a role in her marriage? And so Bill never knew her. Bill only knew the Claire he wanted to have. Quickly, he lowered his head and pressed his mouth onto hers. She remembers the frantic urgency from both of them. His lips were thin and his tongue a restless dancer, pirouetting in her mouth. They went on kissing as if their lives depended on it. She remembers thinking later how his hunger was insatiable and his hands pressed on her back, imprinting themselves on her skin. The jacket slipped off her shoulders. She was warm, so warm that she didn't mind when his cold hands sneaked their way under her jumper and stroked her breasts. He unclasped her bra. She remembers thinking that he didn't need help, not like the first time. Or is she confusing him with someone else later? What does it matter? Kneeling in front of her, he licked her right nipple and rolled the other between his fingertips. Every movement touched the core of her pleasure centre and she was set on fire, dizzy with excitement, lost in a new world. She remembers, and she has remembered many times since, how the anticipation and physical delight took over her whole being and the shed, the rain, all disappeared. Nothing and no one existed but that man kissing her madly. She wished they could be struck by some force that would keep them locked together, like insects preserved in amber. She was hot and wet. She is hot and wet now. She is ready to touch herself, but memories keep flooding in and she doesn't want to let them go lest they disappear forever. Everything happened quickly in the shed. He spread his jacket on the ground and eased her onto it. When he slipped inside her, she came instantly. He moved in and out and she caught his rhythm, feeling waves of orgasms escalating. Her eyes were closed and she was light-headed, her body and mind aware of nothing but the delight of ultimate stimulation, an intensity of sexual excitement she had never known. No one had ever done anything like that to her before. Later, she thought she could have died then and died happy. Her orgasms cascaded one after another and, at some point, he turned her around. He manipulated her body with ease and before she knew it, she was kneeling on all fours on his jacket. He entered her from behind, as an old lover who knew her fantasy, the fantasy she had never dared voice, not even to Patricia. His fingers stroked her thighs, the pressure of their tips gradually sweeping upwards, until they brushed against her swollen lips and slid alongside her clitoris. Sublime. She remembers, her body remembers. He pulled out but his fingers continued to caress her and slowly they moved towards her anus. He licked them and then slid them in, first one, then two, then three. She remembers she could barely stand the excitement and arched her back. He inserted himself between her buttocks, his penis cold and wet. A sharp pain ran through her body, interlaced with pleasure, while he pushed in further into her anus. She squealed and tried to pull away but he held her close and then the pain abated and it was all delight and she pushed back towards him. They waltzed like that, in perfect rhythm, she likes to think. She remembers the feeling of warmth and fullness unlike anything she had experienced before. His fingers played with the rest of her body and she kept pushing backwards to meet him. Later she remembers thinking how they were at one, her body melting into his and she couldn't tell where hers ended and his began. She screamed, unaware and unconcerned but he remained quiet, focused on his task. Eventually, he started groaning and his thrusts became more insistent. Another shuddering orgasm. Has she misremembered? Could it have been that powerful? He held her. Affection displaced cynicism.

But then reality returned as farce. It brings a smile to her face when she thinks of it. She remembers a dog yelping and scratching on the door of the shed. 'Bloody beast, go away,' he shouted but his voice only encouraged the dog to try to break in. The barking became ferocious. A minute later a man stood outside the shed and tried to open the door. Jon held onto the bolt.

'Can you take your dog away,' he shouted. 'We are sheltering from the rain.'

The man said it wasn't raining anymore.

'I know but we can't get out unless you take the animal away.'

'He won't bite you,' the man said.

'I hope he bites you,' Jon mumbled under his breath. 'Why do dog owners expect everyone to like their animals? As if it's not up to me to decide whether I want it near me. They are worse than parents imposing their kids' noise on you. All these sad people needing emotional props and expecting you to tolerate it.' He looked at her, waiting for her to agree. The complaining, the critical Jon, the cynic was back.

At the car park she suggested coffee, but he came up with something about trying to avoid the rush hour traffic. Driving home she had to psych herself not to be angry. Stupid really, she thought later, but at the time, she worried what he took her for. And yet when he rang again, she was happy to hear him.

❧

The third time they met was at the National Gallery, but they didn't look at any pictures together. They had sex in a toilet for the disabled. At sixty-two she was still a prudish little girl and was worried that a pattern had emerged. He was a man who got his kicks from risky situations, she thought. Patricia agreed but couldn't see the problem. 'If it makes him that good, who cares where it happens?' she said. 'Enjoy the sex.'

That was good advice, but she wanted more. She wanted conversation, friendship, something more normal. 'More normal usually comes with bad sex,' Patricia said.

She didn't understand him, or not at the time. Later, she thought that there was nothing to understand. Jon wanted sex and nothing else. She understood Bill. Finding the letter from a surgeon, the letter which had been written a week before their wedding, that letter from a surgeon who, judging by the tone, was a friend, that was a surprise but not a shock. Not a shock because she knew, or at least at the time she believed she knew, that Bill had his reasons. Had she married a different person, he might have spoken to her about it before or even afterwards, but Bill didn't. That was his way. He would have made a decision that was best for both of them. That's what she used to tell herself. Bill loved her, and she trusted him to do the best for her. That's what she believed. Sometimes she asked questions, pointless questions, and she asked them for the sake of asking, he said, and that only annoyed him. It was simpler not to ask; it was easier to trust him.

She understood Zach. She understood Zach better than he understood himself. In a way, it was she who brought him up, help him accept who he was. His Jocasta. No, she had never said that to him. Maybe once she said it to Patricia, who said she was silly to think like that. Patricia said she was jealous. And then laughed. 'Who would have thought,' she said, 'me celibate and you with a lover thirty years younger?' But by that time, it was not the case. She was no longer Jocasta.

She wouldn't ask him but she wonders whether he ever remembers that moment. He couldn't have forgotten but perhaps he doesn't think of it and why should he? That moment in the kitchen or no, it was afterwards, in his little lounge, when after his shower they had that talk. That moment thirty years ago. He cried. He said he had tried and tried and he couldn't do it. What did he mean? He couldn't? But he did, he was hard for hours. 'Injection, I gave myself an injection,' he whispered through tears. A friend of his, a doctor, said older men used them. Why not him if he had a problem. And then he apologised to her. No, he wanted her, yes, he wanted her, it wasn't anything to do with her, he wanted her more than he had ever wanted any woman, but something just didn't work. Something was wrong. And yes, he had slept with the man. The man whose picture she saw fall out of the book he had left on the table. He hated himself for that. What a scene. A man and a woman have sex for hours and then a picture of a naked man pops up, out of the blue. Too much of a coincidence to be plausible in real life. Such bad timing belongs to fiction. But her life often seems to her like the narrative of a novel. What would it be? A Bildungsroman? But how has she developed, what has she learned? That she is a sexual being, and still is. Or a murder mystery? Did she kill her parents, Guillaume, and who knows who else? Bill? Or, is the pattern of her life a romance? Boy gets girl. Girl gets boy. Who did she get accompanying her to the sunset? Bill? A few others to choose from but there was no sunset. She is alone now. Except for her son and his partner. And Martin. Martin who was part of her routine when she was left alone, the routine that saved her until she was ready to break away from it. Martin was hurt then. Hurt because she made it clear to him to abandon his hopes. But she had to do it because she wanted to be kind. Kind to a dear friend. And she loves Martin. Who would have thought they would have lasted this long. Seventy years. A seventy-year-old friendship. But was it kind of him to tell her that Bill needed her more than she needed Bill? So, what if Bill needed a child, had turned her into a child? She too needed a child. Their child. But she has a child now. Things have sorted themselves out.

Smile. She always smiled. 'Smile, Claire,' that's what she has been saying to herself. She was anxious, not as much as Patricia, but she was anxious and scared but she smiled. That book she was supposed to have written. *How to Live to be Ninety.* Or was it, *How to Live to be Ninety and be Happy?* A lovely, kind child she has. A child who is her friend. A child who shares her interests. Her Zach. Her son. She remembers Patricia saying how difficult her daughters could be. One was distant, behaving as if she didn't have a mother, and had no need to see Patricia. The other took offence at everything Patricia said, talked to Patricia as if she were a naughty, little girl. Or no, wasn't it both of them who behaved like that? She remembers Patricia despairing, in tears. She who never cried about anything else. No man made her cry no matter how much she hurt. 'It's different with children,' Patricia used to tell her. 'They can hurt you like no one else can.' She still envied her though. Hurt didn't matter, not that kind of hurt, she thought. If only she could have been a mother, she remembers thinking. She doesn't wish for that now. Perhaps she was spared a great deal of heartache. Besides, she is a mother now. Poor Patricia has been dead for more than twenty, twenty-five years. But it wasn't inevitable things would turn out that way. Lots of parents have close and harmonious relationships with their offspring. Patricia was always anxious, anxious about money, about her private life, about her daughters' health and education. She was always running, always in a hurry. It wasn't easy being a single mother with money tight, at least until her business took off, but perhaps it was her being a distant mother, too impatient, that drove a wedge between her and her children. Perhaps that's why. Oh no, she mustn't fall into that trap. Blame the woman. And the mother in particular.

When the picture fell out of the book, they had that conversation. Zach told her about the injection. That's what they had then, before the blue pill came around, soon after. She gave birth to him then. That's how she thinks of the occasion. He didn't want to be with a man, he told her. He hated himself. But why? 'You are gay, Zach' she said. That was fine. He shook his head and cried. He didn't want to be gay. It's not a question of want. 'You are gay, Zach.' She told him again and again but it took a while for him to accept it. He cried, and she hugged him. A mother and her son then. His Jocasta had left, never to return. But he was blind before, not afterwards. She is getting mixed up now. Yes, Oedipus blinds himself but only when he loses his eyes, can he really see what happened in his life. Zach, she could say, was blind before, not afterwards. She helped him see. She knew he had tried but that was pointless. She felt for him. And she loves him now. She loves him with a depth she could never have reached before. One cannot change such things. One is this or that. Or both. Or nothing. That's what she told him. Yes, he had tried, she knew that. She believed him, of course she did. But why with her, why not with a younger woman. 'You gave me confidence,' he said. And he gave her confidence. But not in the way she gave him confidence. She would never have talked so openly when they sat in the café, straight after they found themselves looking at the book of jazz photographs; she would never have gone with a man she had only just met had he been her age. But a friendly, intelligent man thirty years younger made her feel comfortable. She didn't think much of giving him her number. Until, within days, his seduction process started. He had always liked older women, he told her. Any older woman would do then, she thought. That wasn't flattering. No, they had a lot in common, he hastened to add. He liked talking to her. It was important for him to share interests with a woman. And then, yes. She never said yes, but it happened. She drew a line at being seen in public. They argued about it. She and Bill never argued. She was his 'dear, little Claire' and that was that.

❧

The story of the other meeting, the one that changed her life. How many times would she have heard it? Bill never tired of telling their dinner guests. Some of them, quite a few of them, would have heard it several times. Someone always asked where the two of them had met. 'At an estate agent's,' Bill would say and then wait for the comment. He never volunteered more information. He waited for a comment, a question. For effect. Timing is everything when it comes to having the desired effect on your audience. Bill knew that very well. She had noticed his careful delivery at conferences, always dramatic, changing the tempo, the tone of his voice, the volume. She admired how he manipulated the audience. He knew not just what to say but when and how to say it. And not only at conferences. At the dinner table too. She trusted him. That's why she wasn't upset when she found the letter. Why does she remember it as some kind of a certificate? One doesn't get a certificate for that. In any case, it was mentioned only in passing, a postscript. Scribbled by hand. The chop, the chop, that was the word Bill's colleague used. It took a few minutes for her to work out what it meant. The chop. The rest of the letter was about some patient they shared. She remembers that day because they had a long weekend in Amsterdam to celebrate their fifteenth wedding anniversary and, when they returned, the builder had finished replacing the window in Bill's study. The cleaning lady was ill. She tried agencies, but no one could come on the day and Bill would have needed the study. It was his place for the writing he did at home. It would have upset him to have to work elsewhere. He would have been unhappy with her for not organizing the cleaning. She knew she had to do it herself. She remembers hoovering and the cable getting wrapped around the knob on one of the drawers in the desk and, as she moved around, the drawer was pulled open and some papers fell out. The window was open. A gust of wind blew them around. She collected them and was about to put them back when a piece of paper caught her eye. Dated three weeks before their wedding day, it was written on a typewriter. She sat down, the paper in her hand. Bill's name on it. It made sense. Years and years of thwarted hope made sense. Vasectomy, or the chop, as that doctor wrote. 'Hope the chop is effective.' She sat down on the sofa in the study. She didn't know what to think. Not for five minutes. But then she thought of Bill's love and she understood, made herself understand. He had his reasons, she told herself. She didn't confront him. Some other man might have told his wife, someone else might have wanted to talk about it, before or afterward the procedure, but people are different. Bill was kind and loving and he had his reasons. She didn't tell Patricia either. Not until years later, maybe after Bill was dead. Patricia was shocked. But there was no need for that. The matter was closed; the matter was closed as soon as she discovered it. She understood, and she smiled. She put the paper back in the drawer and she didn't think about it again. She smiled, she forced herself to smile, and she had a smile on when Bill returned home that night. She always smiled. Patricia once said, and she said it completely out of the blue, Patricia said that she should write a book *How to Live to be Ninety and be Happy*. She remembers she laughed and asked her what she could possibly mean. 'You're always smiling,' Patricia said, 'you will live to be ninety.' They couldn't have known how prophetic it was. 'Seriously,' Patricia said 'you should write it. Such a book would be a bestseller.' She thought it was nonsense. She wasn't a writer. If she could have created anything, it would have been a musical composition. But the piece of paper in the study, really, there was nothing to talk about. After all, she was happy with her life. Bill had saved her. That's what Bill's dinner party story was about. Someone always said that an estate agent office didn't sound like a romantic place. The cue for Bill to proceed. 'I agree you wouldn't call it a place where you expect to fall in love. But if you knew the circumstances, you would say our meeting at the estate agent's was truly romantic.' She remembers Bill would stop there, wanting to continue. His sense of timing. Always. There were different-length versions of the account, depending on Bill's mood, his attitude to her, and the composition of the group. Over the years, she heard them all. She remembers Bill started by telling their dinner guests, most of whom were his friends, or rather, his colleagues and professional contacts, that he was sitting in a café opposite the estate agent's, at his usual table, at the usual hour, following his weekly ward consultation, when he saw a young woman, hovering on the edge of the pavement, waiting for the lights to change. There was an air of fragility about her, he would say, and it was not only her slim figure or her pale face, but her whole demeanour which made her resemble a delicate doll. A fine, porcelain doll. She remembers how proud Bill was of his language when he said that. He didn't read much fiction, and no poetry at all – all his time was spent on medicine – but sometimes he liked to show off with a word or phrase he thought sounded poetic. She remembers such moments used to make her smile. He was doing it to please her. She would feel an urge to hug him, the first few times, at least. 'When everyone started crossing the road,' Bill said, 'the woman didn't move, as if she had changed her mind. Moments later, as the green light flashed again, she stepped out, but hesitantly, like someone who is weary of the ground giving way.' She remembers that particular description. It was another description Bill would have enjoyed using, another that he repeated each time. She remembers he said he watched the woman enter the estate agent's. She pushed the door open but she looked unsure whether to go in. He left the cafe and crossed the road. He wasn't following her; he stressed that point, but someone always teased him. How many times had she heard a colleague of his say, 'Come on, Bill. Who are you kidding? A beautiful young woman enters an estate agent shop, and it's only then you remember that you want to sell your house?' She remembers the guests laughing at that point. In a longer version of the story, Bill would tell the table that they would see how lucky it was for everyone that he had, at that instant, decided to sell his property. For some time, he had known that he would have to move house to keep his sanity. He had awful neighbours and he was fed up with their dog barking day and night. She remembers Martin saying later that the neighbour's dog was fiction, plausible fiction, and it was really all about Bill not being able to cope with the memories in that house. But that was Martin's take on Bill's story and it really didn't matter but Martin said it at a time when he was upset with her and it was most unkindly, a very unkind moment. By the time Bill entered the shop, the woman was lying unconscious on the floor by the main desk. He said he could see that the two young men kneeling beside her were in a state of panic; one of them mentioned the recovery position. Not that either of them knew what it meant, Bill would add. An older woman was on the phone to the emergency services. He told them he was a doctor and bent down to attend to the girl. Yes, she remembers, he referred to her as a girl. She was young but for Bill, every woman was a girl. He established that her pulse was rising nicely; he could tell there was nothing serious. She was probably dehydrated, or not eating properly. What with the rationing after the war, maybe she was starved. Apparently, he had another fear, but that one he would admit to her alone, not to the guests: he was worried she might have been pregnant and was pleased when she told him later that it was out of the question. When he raised his eyebrows – hadn't he heard the same story from many a young woman? – she said she thought she was a virgin. 'She thought? That's a strange way of putting it,' he said. She didn't respond, and he felt it better not to ask further what she meant. By that time, they were sitting in the café, at his usual table which had remained unoccupied while he was at the estate agent's. He had led her there so that he could 'keep an eye on her', he said. He kept his eye on her for many years after that. Didn't he say something about a serious abnegation of his professional duties had he left her? It was either the ambulance or him, he insisted. He asked her whether she was looking to buy a home and she told him about the death of her parents and her need to sell their house. She remembers he said later, many years later, that she didn't seem shy, but her answers were curt. He could see she was embarrassed and keen to leave as soon as possible. With his doctor's hat on, he advised her to take it easy, to drink her coffee and several glasses of water. She kept apologising for wasting his time. He assured her he didn't mind. She said she had no idea doctors could be responsible for those who were not their patients. 'But you have just become my patient,' he said and added it would be best if he organised a full health check-up for her but of course, she was free to refuse. She agreed. She remembers being embarrassed to have fainted and not knowing what to say, she remembers that she would have agreed to anything as long as it meant she could leave. Before they parted, she gave him her address and telephone number. She feared it would have seemed impolite to refuse after he had been so caring. He rang her later the same day to check how she was and told her he would collect her for her check-up the next day. Unfailingly, she remembers, as Bill finished, their guests would turn sentimental saying what a lovely story it was and he would say: 'Romantic. Just romantic. If that isn't romantic, I don't know what is.' After she had told him that serendipity was one of her favourite words, a few years into their marriage, and not only because she liked the sound and what it stood for but the history of its genesis, none of which Bill would have known, he started telling their dinner guests that the way they had met was serendipity. And sometimes he added 'it was serendipity, for my dear, little Claire'. She was always his 'dear, little Claire'. There were occasions when a kind guest pointed out, with a smile, always with a smile but she thought there was serious intent, that it was serendipity for Bill too but Bill let it pass. Each time she resolved to raise that with him after the dinner, once they were alone, but she always forgot. But what did it matter? She was happy. Yes. She told herself.

Years later, many years after Bill's death, she began to wonder whether they had met because they were both running away from something, and while escaping, their paths crossed. However, they were hardly running in the same direction. That's not romantic. But the way Bill told their story was. He wanted it to be romantic. Meeting Jon wasn't romantic. That was something else. Her dating, her blind dating wasn't romantic. But she gave it up very quickly. She only met two or three people. The boring lawyer, why does she still remember him, the boring lawyer pontificating about wine, wanting to show her his cellar with its vintage collection. She remembers feeling sorry for him, so sorry that she agreed to meet him in a hotel and there she felt even more sorry for him but, she could never understand how she could be so sorry to lie next to him and do things that she hated doing and then having to comfort him for not being able to get an erection. Why did she feel sorry for him for being pasty, overweight and misshapen? Not to mention his complete lack of self-awareness. She pitied him for that. He may have had a wine cellar, and who knows what else, but to be so unprepossessing and so unaware of it. She couldn't understand that. The memory of his yellowing toenails still gives her shivers. Despite all his wealth, he never bothered to have a pedicure.

She should have trusted her first impression and told him immediately that there was no chance of anything between them. The ring was the first giveaway, a signet ring and she should have listened to her instinct. But she knew it was prejudice, an irrational aversion, and awareness of her prejudices always made her feel guilty. Patricia agreed with her. Signet rings and beards were no no. Tattoos were beyond the pale. All her prejudices, but at least she was aware of them. Why did men think – maybe they still do – beards were attractive? She remembers Patricia saying that there were a few she could have tolerated. A few who had other qualities. For Patricia, Fidel Castro was one of the exceptions. She used to laugh at Patricia's 'if I could meet him, I would forgive him his beard'. But with the lawyer, guilt led her to be nice to him and ignore the ring. What was it she disliked about signet rings? Was it their pretence, displaying the family crest. Or was it that they were ugly? Yes, they were ugly. She has never seen one she liked. You couldn't imagine an architect wearing one. Architects she had known, such as her friend Charles, her friend from her student days, were stylish. Charles always wore dark trousers and a white shirt. Simple and stylish. Bill had a signet ring when they met. She remembers noticing it in the café after her fainting fit and thinking how horrible it was. She found it difficult to keep her eyes off the ring, like the sickening sight of a squashed bird or a pile of vomit that one cannot stop staring at. That ring was particularly ugly, not just the head but the shank and especially the part of the shank next to the head, the triangular bit. Before she could agree to marry him, she told him how she felt about the signet ring. She remembers thinking at the time how brave she was. But silly, really. She should have told him about a lot of other things she disliked. No, that's not fair. There was not so much she objected to at the time but there were a few issues. But something stopped her. What? Her shyness? The reluctance of a child to criticize a parent? As for the signet, Bill indulged her. He took it off on the spot and never wore it again. He said it didn't mean much to him. It wasn't a family heirloom; he had bought it for himself before his first marriage. How bizarre, she remembers thinking. She wonders what happened to the ring? It wasn't there with his stuff after his death. She remembers sorting out Bill's study, a year or two after he died. She had not been able to bring herself to do it before, couldn't do it before because of her fear, her fear of finding more about those secret visits, more of the stuff that Dr Williams was up to. Dr Williams, the character in Martin's novel. And when she did clear his desk, yes, there were a few numbers and some names, Annabelle and Christelle and the like, the sort of names women doing that sort of thing used, their stage names as it were. She feared anything she discovered might hinder her mourning. But then when she did find phone numbers and a few cards, yes, Christelle had a card with a drawing of stockings and a suspender belt, she pushed it to the back of her mind. She didn't think of it. Once she heard someone make a reference to the adventures of Victorian gentlemen, and it crossed her mind that, in many ways, Bill was a Victorian gentleman in a way, in many ways even though he didn't live in the period. But she didn't find the ring and she wondered what he had done with it. She remembers she came across a photo of Bill and his wife with the baby, a little boy who died at three weeks from a congenital heart defect. The parents were smiling. She remembers holding it in her hand and feeling like an intruder into a private family moment. She remembers thinking how all three of them were dead and how, had the baby not died, the woman would not have killed herself and her own life would have been different. She wouldn't have married Bill and she might have been with someone else, or perhaps no one, or she might have had a child. But that was pointless speculation, and yes, her thoughts often wandered in the direction of pointless speculation. What if . . . , what if . . . ? She kept the picture. She felt she had no right to, but there was no one to give it to and it felt wrong to dispose of it. One day, Zach and Gabriel will find it and they will have to deal with the picture of three people about whom they know nothing. Perhaps Gabriel might use it in a story. Yes, she should talk to him about it. It would please her if the dead woman and her baby were given a voice, a kind of life. But she didn't find the ring. Bill might have given it to someone. She once asked Martin and he had no idea. But Martin said there was a story there, a missing signet ring and he said he would use the idea. He did, he told her a year later.

But with that oenological lawyer, harping on about his cellar full of vintage bottles, perhaps it was all about her wanting to give it a go, having let herself be persuaded by Patricia that agency dating was more straightforward than a conventional meeting as everyone was explicit about who they were and what they wanted. But were they? And even if they were, most men she had contacted, and the few she had met, had an exaggerated sense of what they were offering and equally what they were expecting. It felt like a market, people selling themselves, many of them shamelessly. But Patricia never seemed to lose faith. Despite her fear of death, she was an eternal optimist. A single mum, abandoned by her husband, well, he sounded like a genuine bastard, didn't keep in touch with the children, never paid anything for them. And yet, she was keen to meet a man to share her life and had so much faith in dating. But that was Patricia. So different from her. She couldn't have carried on with all those messages and meetings. Too nerve-wracking, too time-consuming. And for what? She wasn't sure. It was Jon, meeting Jon, missing what she had experienced with him that made her think there might be someone out there. But there wasn't. Not with the dating agencies. There were many odd people, like that serial dater Patricia spotted straight away. He had a standard message with a picture and as the years passed, he recycled the message but updated the photo. At least that was honest. Patricia heard from him three times over the years. The third time she had registered under an assumed name because she had sussed him out and wanted to check her suspicion was right. It seemed that as soon as a new woman appeared on the list of the agency, he would send his standard package. He must have been writing a dozen messages every day. After a couple of weeks of exchanging letters, which would rapidly grow in intensity, he would declare his love for the woman. He carried on writing until the woman reciprocated with her confession of love and then he disappeared, ignoring all her messages. He was a translator, or a proof-reader, on some remote Scottish island. He must have been desperately lonely with very little human contact and would have devised the game to keep himself sane. Was it innocuous? Selfish, certainly. Using women's affection to spice up his own sad life without caring if he hurt them. He seemed an extreme case but it didn't take her long to notice that most people using dating agencies were either lonely or sad, or both. But that man was insensitive. All he wanted was power and control over the poor sod writing to him.

He had no longing in his soul. She remembers reading a story, a story by a French writer, about a woman describing her relationship with a man in minute detail, recounting years of love, the ups and downs of the relationship, only for the reader to realise gradually that the man didn't exist. The woman longed to love someone who existed only in her imagination. That was true longing, she remembers thinking. Patricia was like that. She was in love with a man who didn't exist. She died never finding love. She remembers Patricia saying the best man would be like a monster stitched by Dr Frankenstein: the brain from one, the body from another, the character from yet another and so on. But perhaps she was too much of an idealist. She might have been happier had she settled for a compromise. Most people do. She did. Did she? Yes, she did but without knowing at the time it was a compromise.

She misses Patricia.

And then there was the concert, a few years after Jon, just after she had given up dating. Patricia was to go with her but her mother wasn't well and she had to rush to Scotland. Martin joined her. She remembers being surprised at his willingness to come with her since he never went anywhere, apart from walking Poirot in the local park or nipping to the shops. By that time he was even more of a recluse than before. She remembers him joking that, since it was at St Martin's, he had to go. She remembers Martin sitting on one side of her and a man arriving with two women. The man sat next to her. As soon as she saw him, she was struck by his face, rugged, slightly bohemian, artistic even. She struggled to describe it, but it was an unconventional face which intrigued her so much that she began to fear missing the opportunity of making contact. The thought that she would never see him again was painful, viscerally painful. While listening to the music, her thoughts were focused on how she could start a conversation with the man, how she could exchange some information with him, the kind of information, even if it were not his telephone number or address, the kind of information that would allow her to find him later. They looked at each other a few times and she shared her programme with him, having placed it on the shelf of the pew in front of them. She remembers that he had a large coat and was trying to bundle it into the space below the shelf in front of them, but the coat proved unruly and kept unfolding itself, fidgeting around, and slipping to the floor. The man picked it up and repeated the process. She remembers thinking of it as a dialogue between the coat and the man, a game. She was amused and, best of all, it gave her an opportunity to meet the man's eyes. Whenever the coat moved, they looked at each other and smiled. A sense of complicity. Togetherness. The two of them in a game against the coat. They couldn't have spoken since the music was playing. As the interval arrived, the man vanished with the two women. She had missed her opportunity to establish contact. She remembers thinking that since he had two women with him, it was possible that neither of them was his partner. They would have all been friends, she tried to tell herself. The concert was nearing the end and yet she didn't know how to approach the man, how to find out something about him that would help her trace him later. She couldn't allow him simply to disappear into the London crowd. She had to see him again. For the first time in her life, she had a specific sexual fantasy involving a man about whom she knew nothing at all. When the music finished, and the encore was over, they were putting their coats on, and she asked the man whether he was a writer. It was a silly question. She had uttered the words without planning what to say. He said he wasn't. She asked whether he was an artist. He carried an air of bohemia, with his androgynous haircut and unconventional clothes. No, he was a scientist. And then, she blurted out, and for the rest of her life she was glad she did, she blurted out that she would like to see him again. He smiled; he had a smile on his face, most of the time, she remembers, but the smile broadened. His eyes smiled, and they smiled with amazement. He asked her whether she had a telephone number. She wrote it down and they parted. She remembers on the way home thinking that she should have asked for his telephone number too because now she had to wait for him to contact her and perhaps he would not. Before they set out on the way home, while they were still standing in the pew, putting on their coats and wrapping their scarves around, yes, she remembers it was a cold January evening, Martin made a comment about her not wasting any time. His voice betrayed a mixture of anger and disappointment. It pained her to hurt him. She remembers saying that something was telling her that she had to see that man again. That was the truth. Her longing to see the man again pervaded her body. It was not a longing of the mind. Never before, or after, had she experienced pain in her body at the thought of missing another person. She didn't say any of that to Martin because she knew he would not understand. Nor would she have wanted to upset him further. But he mumbled something about her not being fair to him, flirting with another man while she was in his company and she remembers feeling sorry but she knew she had had to act as she did. She wanted to say that he was a friend, like Patricia was a friend and had she been with her, she wouldn't have minded but this was before she and Martin had their frank chat, when things between them were still unclear and unsaid, at least as far as he was concerned. She was always clear about her feelings. Another few months passed after the concert before she told him how she felt uncomfortable about his arm around her while they were watching a film and sitting on the sofa, and how she didn't like him always asking where she was going and who with. But that night after the concert, Martin was quiet on the way home and she remembers unlocking her door and rushing to check her messages on the phone, hoping that the man would have contacted her. She remembers the sadness, the shock even, when she realised that she had written down the wrong telephone number, a telephone number that didn't exist, a number that was a combination of her two telephones: mobile and landline. She remembers thinking whether she could try to change her telephone number but was told it was not possible. She remembers thinking how stupid she had been.

❧

She hasn't had that dream now for several years but for a long time it used to recur. Would it still frighten her? It's been forty-odd years since his death. What used to puzzle her about the dream was that in it Bill didn't complain about her driving, as he used to on most occasions. Or perhaps in the dream it was the days after Bill's stroke, yes, she thinks it was, and by that time he had no choice but to put up with her driving. Not that there was anything wrong with her driving. Bill had his own style and hers was different. That's all that would have bothered him. He wanted everyone to do things his way. She did speak to Zach about the dream, yes, they talked about it at length. Of course, they did. Her own psychologist. She can't remember everything he said except that the dream was a classic expression of the dreamer's sadness and guilt. Guilt? 'Well,' Zach said, 'who knows what kind of guilt.' Possibly guilt that she had survived her husband. That she has had a good life and he had no chance of sharing it. Anyway, it was Bill who had insisted on taking the pills. She thought he had already taken them, but she didn't wish to argue. He always said he was right.

❧

She remembers telling Patricia about the young man, a builder, who wouldn't leave her alone. It was silly of her, but she was inexperienced with blind dating, any dating for that matter; she was caught off guard and she gave him her telephone number. And then he kept ringing, trying to persuade her to meet him, wanting to book a hotel. And her telling him that she couldn't meet a man so much younger, thirty years younger than her and him saying how he had always loved older women which was another thing that put her off. She was an older woman. Of course, at sixty-four, she was an older woman to a thirty-year old man, but there was no need for him to spell it out. And then him ringing back to present his trump card. She remembers him bragging about the size of his cock and that was the final straw. A big one was the final straw, not to mention the language. Cock. She hates the word. So vulgar. But, a big one was the final straw. Has she just thought that? A funny sentence. Hah. Not funny. Stupid really. Why do men assume that the size is so important? Patricia teased her. She remembers Patricia laughing. 'When did you ever have a builder ringing you back?' But no, she was a snob and she admitted it. No builders. She remembers wondering out loud what they would talk about and Patricia laughing even more. What would they talk about? They would fuck. She could be coarse. Zach was the same age as the builder when they met. But they had a lot to talk about. And they didn't meet through a dating agency. And he wasn't a builder. She remembers thinking how exhilarating it was talking to a young person who was knowledgeable about classical music. When he said they should get a coffee, she was flattered but nothing sexual crossed her mind. No, how could it have? He was so young. They sat down and talked for another hour. It seemed natural to give him her number. She never hesitated. She remembers thinking he wasn't trying to pick her up. He rang a day later and suggested a concert but she wasn't free. Instead, they met over lunch to 'catch up and talk music', as he said. Afterwards, he invited her to his flat to peruse his collection of old LPs. He was, and still is, a big jazz fan and it was a revelation to listen to his records. She even dabbled with a few arrangements herself. By then, she knew who he was, where he worked and so on and was fairly confident he wasn't an axe murderer. Nor did she suspect him to be interested in her as a woman. She remembers she was taken aback the first time he made a move to kiss her but there was something so tender and beautiful, tentative, even shy about him as he touched her, she was moved. She responded.

She didn't tell Patricia, not until much later. Perhaps she was ashamed; no, not ashamed but she would have feared Patricia teasing her. Their lovemaking was gentle and exploratory. He didn't have much experience and that suited her. With Bill she didn't know what she liked and accepted whatever was on offer, and with Jon it was him leading the proceedings, and her delighting in what she discovered. But with Zach, she felt open to express her own desires. She remembers being grateful for the dimmed lights and realising that he was equally shy undressing in front of her. She remembers agonising over what she called the corporeal anxiety of the older woman. Later, after she had supported Zach to come out, and spilled the beans to Patricia, whose first thoughts were Joan Collins, Madonna and Brigitte Macron, she remembers wishing she had their self-confidence. In their place, she would have been beset by constant anxiety how to make herself appear younger. She couldn't sustain a relationship in which she was forever worried about looking old. 'Men don't care about their ageing bodies when they have much younger partners, why should we?' Patricia said. Why indeed? But she was too self-conscious of her skin, which had lost its elasticity, of her body, slim but soft and wobbly, of her muscles dissolving into soft dough. Perhaps she was too vain, or too screwed up, as Patricia said. Both were true but she couldn't think of anyone who wasn't, if not vain at least screwed up. Better things came out of that relationship. After all these years, Zach is still one of the most important, no, he is the the most important person in her life, the most important person of her entire life. Her beautiful son.

But there was Bill who saved her, or so he said and she believed him. When their dinner guests heard the story of their meeting, someone always said that Bill was a knight in shining armour who saved a damsel in distress. It was a good story for a dinner party, a story that presented their marriage as a fairy tale and that put everyone around the table in good mood. It was Bill's story, a story in which she was a passive, unconscious participant, literally unconscious and brought back to life, woken up. Pity he didn't need to give her the kiss of life. That would have been an even better story for the amusement of their dinner guests. Now she wishes she had known how to tell her version of the story of their meeting but that was not possible, not during their marriage. His story was the only story at the time. She had heard it innumerable times and it had imprinted itself on her mind. She saw that day and all the days of their marriage as Bill saw them. And she was content. She was happy. Or that's what she thought. It didn't occur to her to think differently. As time passed and their respective roles of the knight in shining armour and the damsel in distress became further entrenched, the possibility of an alternative point of view, the sense that there could have been other, underlying narratives, faded away. But what did it matter? She had found a life with a man who was good to her from the moment he set eyes on her. Well, that's what he used to remind her.

She remembers an occasion when she was anxious about something, maybe it was another month of expectations thwarted, or she had a headache, she cannot remember, but she said and she could not understand why she said it, the words just came out, she said that Bill was her Pygmalion. Bill breathed life into her. There was a moment of silence at the table, and when the conversation resumed, no one commented on what she had said. She remembers being relieved, when she thought about it afterwards, relieved that no one who might have known of the myth had picked up on what she said. Her words were lost in the cacophony of small talk. It was silly of her to mention a myth she disliked, a myth that she always considered a male myth, a myth about men exerting power over women, a myth about a man creating a woman as an object according to his desires. A man giving life to a woman who was no more than his object, an object made to measure, his measure. Why would she have wanted anyone to see her as the woman in that myth? Because she had unconsciously absorbed Bill's story, she thought later. Yes, she was a lifeless creature for those few seconds as she lay unconscious on the floor of the estate agents and, after that, life returned to her, Bill gave her life, but then she was lost, as Bill said, a 'lost, little girl' but that was temporary, she is sure she would have managed on her own. She would have found herself. And she did. She ran the house single-handedly. But that was not the life she had chosen. Her life was decided for her. Besides, during the marriage, it never occurred to her that she was capable of living independently and doing what she wanted. Bill said she was lost and that was the truth she believed in. And then there was his omniscience, his professional success, the adulation of his team, his unshakeable faith in the rightness of his decisions. She recalls the day when Patricia lost her temper and told her to stop thinking of herself as a lost, little girl. She didn't behave like that, why did she accept being referred to as such? It was quite an outburst and she remembers being taken aback. Her first thought was that Patricia only said it because she didn't like Bill. And how she defended him in front of her friend, telling Patricia that she was being unfair, that she didn't know how much Bill did for her, how he had saved her from loneliness and misery. But such sentiments only enraged Patricia even further. She told her she was talking nonsense. What misery? What loneliness? She was an intelligent, good-looking, young woman, she could have done whatever she wanted, she could have had anyone she chose to.

But it's true that she was young and pliable and he was more than twenty years older, set in his ways. She slotted herself into his lifestyle, his timetable, his daily and annual routine like a new child into a family, a child who doesn't know anything else. Of course she accepted Bill's ways. She was a well brought up young woman, taught to respect her elders. She recalls Bill saying how glad he was to have been in that café on that day and to have gone to the estate agent at the time when she was there and how wonderful it was that he could help her. And she was grateful to him. But he was wrong to think that she was a *tabula rasa*, that she was a 'lost, little girl'. Ten years after his death, she realised that throughout their marriage she was barely aware that there was something more that she wanted, something that flickered, flickered faintly at the back of her mind, vague and unfelt most of the time but, occasionally, that unknown desire threw a faint light on her life, reminding her of its presence, nibbling at her existence. It took her a long time to realise that the fainting fit hadn't erased the legacy of her upbringing, or her ambitions and hopes. It took her years to remember that throughout her teens, she used to see her future as a professional musician, probably a concert pianist. She remembers that she imagined a life dedicated to her art. She knew it would require a great deal of sacrifice, but she didn't mind that. She wanted to be a successful concert pianist and was prepared to do whatever it took to achieve her ambition. But perhaps, and she will never know, perhaps Bill saved her from having to face her lack of talent, most likely her mediocrity, even her lack of discipline. And somewhere in that plan for her future, there was a desire, a strong, visceral desire for a child, maybe more than one.

She and Bill were married barely six months after the meeting at the estate agent's. She remembers him organising the wedding and saying it was best to have a small celebration, not much fuss, and that was fine with her. She didn't know what to think about small or large weddings. She remembers inviting two friends from university, one arrived with her boyfriend, and there were a few of Bill's colleagues. She can smile now as she remembers that everyone present assumed that the haste of the wedding meant she was pregnant and, while no one said anything directly, she could feel their eyes on her, looking for the tell-tale bump. One woman from Bill's lab even gently patted her on her tummy and said she would soon have her hands full. When she remembers those days, she knows that if she had been confused, if she had been a 'lost, little girl', it was the marriage that turned her that way.

She remembers the day after the wedding: she was left alone to create a home. That's what Bill said when he left early in the morning. He would come back late and he expected to see progress with her turning their new house into a comfortable home. He never voiced his expectations explicitly, but she remembers she felt them, she knew she had to do it to please him and she wanted to please him. She wanted him to be happy. Years later, she realised that she could have employed a cleaner and a gardener and paid someone to advise on décor but, at the time, she had no idea how to go about the role that had been thrust upon her. After all, she had been brought up to study and work on her music. Her mother never allowed her to do anything at home, saying that she was too young, with too much potential, to waste her life on domestic trivia. And then, newly married, in a big, empty house that required modernisation, she had no idea where to start. She spent long days doing everything herself, everything she could manage, and agonizing over decisions of style. She could do the house as she liked, but she was not sure what she liked. And even when her taste in décor began to develop, she was unsure about many of her decisions but had no one to consult. Bill made it clear that he didn't want to be bothered with domestic issues. He was too busy at work. And yet she knew that he would complain if he didn't like the colour of a rug or the pattern of a lampshade. It was up to her to choose the furniture but she had to guess what he liked. She made mistakes, and days would pass without her even lifting the lid of the piano. She remembers the day when she realised that a career as a concert pianist, or even a professional musician, had slipped out of her reach. She remembers waking up as Bill was making the tea in the kitchen, getting ready to leave for work, and she remembers the sense of anxiety and tightening in her chest as she realised how many tasks were waiting for her to address, and then it hit her that it wasn't those tasks that were the problem because as soon as the renovations were completed, there wouldn't be so much to do in the house and she would be able to practice piano for hours. But being an artist is not a nine to five job, being an artist is living like an artist, thinking like an artist. And such a lifestyle was no longer possible for her. Her realisation came that morning, as she was listening to an interview with a musician she admires, a musician who lived with another musician and who said that they both lived solely for music. Their home is chaotic but they don't mind, the musician said. Bill would return home tired and he expected a comfortable, stress-free environment. It fell to her to provide it. She didn't complain. She accepted it without a trace of resentment. After the first year, the house was in a reasonable shape, and she returned to her music. She found time to play every day, though not much, and to go to concerts once a week but the only career in music that was still possible in her circumstances was to teach. That was a huge step down from what she used to dream about but she accepted her lot. At least she was maintaining a home for Bill and their children. She could look forward to becoming a mother. But years passed and it didn't happen. Medically, nothing seemed wrong with either of them. It was 'just one of those things'. She read about women spending years trying to get pregnant and then achieving their dream once they no longer expected it to happen. All she needed was to relax and it would happen, she remembers thinking. She tried. She accepted her childlessness. But it didn't happen. Bill was kind, always kind and understanding. She cried on his shoulder. He would reassure her that they were happy. Yes, it would have been good to have had a child but at least they had each other, he said. He was always kind. She was his 'dear Claire', she was his 'little Claire' and she didn't have to worry about big decisions. She travelled with him to conferences and was pleased to hear again and again how many people in different parts of the world heaped praise on his professional achievements. There was something thrilling to watch Bill give a talk with his unimpeachable authority and to know his intimate, vulnerable side, his fear of disorder, his obsession with punctuality, his phobia of pigeons. With time, she came to appreciate what marrying him meant for her and she grew to love him.

❧

Hers was a mature love, a caring love, a love that one could rely on to last, a love that couldn't be dented by a passing infatuation with someone you come across in your daily life, she used to tell herself. She remembers from time to time meeting someone who was kind and whom she liked. But no, not more than that. She remembers the artist, a painter she met at a secondary school, when they had received a grant to develop an art project with socially disadvantaged children. She had seen the advertisement for a collaborator and applied, thinking it would be good for her to be in touch with young people. The painter, Lucca, yes, unusually, how she remembers that, unusually, he spelt his name with a double 'c', yes, Lucca was an attractive man she thought and she remembers being flattered by his interest in her, the way a smile hovered around his lips when he talked to her, an almost involuntary smile, a smile that couldn't be stopped, a smile telling her that he liked her, liked her as a woman. And she admired his passion for painting. A passion for art could be a turn on. She only realised that later in life, much later, after she became a widow. She remembers the buzz when they discussed exhibitions during breaks. Or was it a frisson? She remembers meeting him once at a gallery because they were developing a session around a picture and they went there to make notes; it felt like a date, it felt like a date because they met outside their place of work, and that was exciting, but worrying too, yes, somewhere at the back of her mind it worried her. She remembers not wishing to acknowledge it to herself, but it worried her how much she liked him. She remembers another time he asked her to join him for an exhibition that she didn't think was relevant to their project; she made up some excuse about a previous engagement. She was afraid of seeing him again.

She remembers fearing that she might be too weak, that she might like him too much. Lucca gave her a copy of a children's book with his illustrations. He said he hoped one day to read it to his children. And he said he hoped she would do the same. No, she couldn't have been interested in Lucca. She couldn't love anyone but her husband. Or that's what she thought then. Bill was her life. Patricia said they were the only couple she could think of who had remained faithful throughout their marriage. 'Or at least, you did,' she would add. She didn't like hearing 'or at least you did'. She was sure Bill was faithful to her. She could never imagine him with any other woman. Patricia said she shouldn't be so sure. 'You never know.' True, but with Bill, she thought, she was sure. He never even looked at other women, barely seemed to notice them. She remembers sometimes pointing out a beautiful woman to him and he would glance in her direction and shrug. He was too preoccupied with his work to consider having an affair, she used to think. Patricia said she hoped she was right. She was sure she was. But then there came a day when she wasn't so sure, but it didn't matter. Those were not affairs. Anyway, she was happy, she told herself.

She must still have the book that Lucca gave her. Yes, it is on a shelf in her music room. She will take it down and leaf through. Perhaps he did read the story to his child. Her copy has never been read by any child. She remembers thinking of giving it to Patricia's first grandchild, Alba, the girl who was twelve when she accompanied her mother and they found Patricia lying dead on the floor in the hall. She kept in touch with the daughters for a while, mostly Christmas cards, and she thinks that she saw Alba in the paper the other day. Alba, a woman with a beautiful name. She remembers mentioning the name to Patricia's daughter, years before she fell pregnant with the girl who was to be called Alba. She had run into her and Patricia while shopping, nothing special, groceries probably, and then Patricia was stopped by someone else and she and the daughter were left alone. She doesn't remember why in the middle of a supermarket, holding a trolley, she would tell Patricia's daughter about her favourite name, for a girl, that is. Perhaps they talked about Pound. Yes, Patricia's daughter was an English undergraduate – at Sussex, was it? – and Pound came up. And his 'Alba'. 'As cool as the pale wet leaves of the lily-of-the-valley / She lay beside me in the dawn.' Yes, she recited the poem to Patricia's daughter while they were both leaning on their respective shopping trollies next to the vegetable display. She had heard the poem turned to music. But Patricia's daughter didn't know the poem and said she would look it up. She must have. And then a few years later, she called her first-born child Alba. How wonderful, she thought. Patricia said the name was nice, but it sounded pretentious. She didn't tell her that she might have given the idea to the daughter. But she didn't really influence her. She only introduced her to the poem. Could Alba be a journalist? There was an article about nutrition and health, yes, Alba Perone-Smith, she remembers. It must have been her.

But the picture book, the picture book from Lucca was about a young girl who wants to be a painter and who loves going to galleries where she copies Picasso, Matisse and Modigliani. There has been no child to read her copy. She had felt too emotional about the book to pass it on to Alba. But she is happy. She remembers the happiness, the happiness she still enjoys, of going places with Zach, or with Zach and Gabriel, and people assuming, sometimes even saying it, that she was the mother of one of them, and the years of happiness of being a mother and not just a mother but the mother of a lovely young man. The lovely young man, her son, who is now sixty-two, the age she was when she met him. How that used to worry her then. How that prevented her from going anywhere with Zach. For the first few months, she agreed to meet him only in his flat. She feared being taken for Zach's mother. She feared people's judgement.

Jocasta. An older woman with a young man is often seen as a seductress, incestuous even, a cradle snatcher. They argued about it. She remembers Zach wanting them to go out for a meal and her fearing that the waiter would automatically present her with the bill, as he would assume she was taking her son for a treat. She remembers him pleading with her to go with him to parties. He asked again and again. She remembers how upset he was when she refused to accompany him to what he called an informal gathering in a gallery where a friend of his was celebrating the completion of a documentary. Zach argued that no one would know the two of them were together. She remembers him saying they could arrive separately, but it would have given him lots of pleasure to talk to her at the event and he really wanted her to meet some of his friends. She remembers asking him how he would introduce her, and he said he hadn't thought about it. 'A friend of your mother's,' she remembers saying and having to apologise. Zach didn't have a mother. She walked out when he was five years old, and he was brought up by his grandparents. But they are all in the past, their arguments. And now, for her, everything is in the past. No, that's unfair, she mustn't complain, she mustn't feel sorry for herself. There is nothing to be sorry about. And she has no regrets. Zach has no parents. Unless his mother is still alive, alive but as good as dead. He is an orphan. She was orphaned at twenty. And Gabriel's parents died from cancer, one after the other. That was before she knew him. So, they are all orphans. And Martin. But at which age do you stop being an orphan? No, Martin can't be an orphan, not at a hundred and two. Nor her at ninety-two. What about the boys? In their sixties? No, they have her. They are not orphans.

But later, going out together was fine, it was a pleasure, a delight, the greatest happiness she has ever known. She was no longer Jocasta. And there were days when he cried on her shoulder. But that's what mothers are for. Martin warmed to him straight away. She remembers being apprehensive about how he would react to this young man around her. She remembers inviting both of them for dinner. Not that Martin needed inviting, he was eating supper with her most evenings, but when Zach arrived for the first time it was a special occasion. She had talked to Martin about Zach before. She had told him how they met but Martin still asked again, in front of Zach, as if he wasn't sure whether to believe her. But the evening went better than she could have hoped. Zach, always caring Zach, did his homework. He had read two of Martin's recent novels and Martin was impressed. He took to him. Had anyone watched from the side, they wouldn't have believed it was the first time all three of them were together. She remembers them walking Zach to the Tube afterwards and Poirot running ahead and then coming back and ignoring her and Martin, always coming back to Zach. A family with a dog.

Zach's ups and down. She remembers those. Heartache for years until she introduced him to Gabriel. That was serendipity. She was contacted by the council asking whether she would be prepared to answer questions for some research project into the memorials people created for their deceased. She had paid for a memorial bench for Patricia and that's why they had her details. It was Gabriel who turned up to talk to her. At the time, he had a part-time job with a polling organisation. She remembers she liked him straight away, and they carried on talking after they had been through the questions. He told her he was writing a novel, his second but the first hadn't been published. The main character was a psychologist. She told him she had a good friend who was a psychologist, but he didn't respond to that and then she added that they were the same age and when he still didn't show interest, she said it might be useful for him to meet her friend and she proceeded to talk about Zach's work with torture victims. Gabriel didn't seem impressed, but she pressed on. How right she was. Something told her to carry on, some sixth sense and, eventually, Gabriel agreed to meet her again and be introduced to her friend. How many times has he thanked her since? How many times in almost thirty years?

Gabriel, her lovely son-in-law. Her novelist son-in-law.

His novels have intriguing covers, works of art in themselves. She prefers editions that have no pictures on the cover, classical, minimalist, *à la* Gallimard, or Fitzcarraldo. All titles with the same plain cover and easily recognisable. But if you are to have a cover, it ought to be designed with care and a great deal of thought. She remembers hearing a publisher saying they were proud to be making books like works of art.

One of Gabriel's novels carries a drawing by Lucian Freud. She recalls that she was familiar with the image but could not tell where she had seen it before. And now, after all these years of not being able to tell, now she knows. The drawing was hanging on the wall opposite the double doors in the lounge of Jon's Soho flat. What a small world. How did the publisher get hold of it? She remembers checking the information on the dust sleeve about the cover of the novel and it said the drawing was in a private collection. She would never have thought it was Jon's. As she ages, many things disappear, and she doesn't know whether to regret that or not but others appear. Like this one. A sudden memory. A sudden realisation. Yes, she remembers standing in the lounge and looking at the drawing while waiting for Jon to come out of the shower. Moving to the window, she thought how that part of London had not changed for more than a century and she almost expected to see Virginia Woolf crossing the Square. That flat later featured in a recurrent dream where a doctor, an Oxford Professor, Mrs Jon, came home early from a conference in America and she remembers she was all mumsy in appearance – why did she look mumsy? – mumsy but also forbidding, with large breasts, wearing a flowery dress and a hat, an old fashioned hat, bizarrely, and this woman had walked in on her in the lounge. The woman immediately realised what had been going on and from the way the woman was speaking, it was clear that it was not the first time she had walked in on her husband and a lover and in the dream she would think how lucky it was that the woman hadn't turned up earlier when Jon had asked her to whip him or even worse when he had made her pee over him. And the woman spoke to her in histrionic tones, in fact, she is not sure whether the woman was wearing a flowery dress or an old-fashioned suit with the waist cinched in, one of those tweed outfits that Lady Bracknell would wear. In fact, the woman looked like Lady Bracknell, yes, she remembers now, and her tone was one of supercilious mockery. How horrible that was. And yes, it's coming to her now, there was a hat with a feather, a trilby with a large feather sticking out. She remembers the woman looking her up and down and then saying that Jon must have lowered his standards or was losing his touch. She remembers the dream following her for months, if not years, after their last meeting, the last meeting in which he told her about his wife and their mostly separate lives and said that all he could offer was sex but he didn't know how long that would work for both of them and he asked for discretion and he said he wished to see her again if she could accept his situation. She wasn't sure and, surprise, surprise, Patricia advised her to agree and take what was good and enjoy it as long as it lasted. But she didn't. She thought she would but then she couldn't. She couldn't allow herself to be reduced to a body to be fucked and it wasn't a question of a relationship, of coming out in public, no, that was not what she was after; it wasn't a question of not being discreet, but it was a question of being reduced to a body to be fucked. If only they could have the occasional coffee, or if they could have eaten out together sometimes, or seen an exhibition, anything, but there was nothing except sex. No, she couldn't do it. It was getting her down, it was undermining her confidence as a woman. And that dream, that dream persecuted her for years. But was it only a dream, can she be sure it was only a dream, because sometimes that scene with Dr Jon/ Lady Bracknell seems so vivid and she cannot be sure that it hadn't happened.

If she had to be reduced to a body to be fucked, she could do it herself. And she did. Patricia couldn't believe it when she told her that Bill had given her a vibrator but then she thought about it and said he was probably abnegating from his role. She cannot remember, and she didn't think about it at the time, but later she realised that she never had an orgasm with him. Partly, she had created a problem by faking her orgasms. She remembers reading that many women do. She wanted to please him and, besides, she thought that it was her fault for not feeling anything but, every now and then, increasingly often, she wanted him to stop. She remembers wanting him to stop because he was hurting her. She wished she had helped him understand what she might find exciting. But she was too shy, or perhaps not shy but unaware that it was something she could have said. Not that she knew what excited her. And he never asked. He had his ways, of course. A man in his mid forties, as he was when they met, a man of that age had his ways of doing things, his way of loving and his way of living. She was young and as he said she was lost, 'my dear, little Claire' was lost. But is that why she adjusted without protesting, is that why she always accepted what he wanted? No, not because she was lost but because he kept telling her that she was lost. She doesn't remember ever initiating sex. She doesn't think Bill expected her to. He certainly never said that she should, that he would like her to. As years passed, they made love less and less frequently and then it stopped altogether. In the last ten years of Bill's life, there was nothing. Only her vibrator. A new one. She bought it herself when the first one from Bill went kaput. She always came with the vibrator. It was quick and powerful, the current running down her body and exiting through her feet. Why feet? That's how it was with the best ones. More intense than anything she could have imagined. Sometimes she felt lonely afterwards and wished there was someone to share the intimacy. But there were benefits. No other person to worry about and accommodate. No other person to listen to. No time to waste. Clean and efficient. Virtual love making. A bit like friendships on Facebook. There but not there.

❧

She remembers that he always took his medication before dinner. It was part of his routine. Or most of it, except for the pills which required him to eat something beforehand. After the stroke, there were quite a few pills but, as always, Bill was well organised. He kept all the medication in a pretty basket in his bathroom. He also had one of those plastic, see-through boxes, each compartment labelled with a day of the week. That evening, she remembers Bill coming to the kitchen with his pills in his hand and filling up a glass of water. At dinner, he had not been talkative, quite grumpy, in fact, but that was not unusual. For years he had been grumpy with her and the grumpiness only got worse after the stroke. They had a glass of wine each, or Bill might have had more than one, and afterwards, as she was going to the kitchen, taking the dishes, Bill asked her to bring him his pills. He had already poured himself a large glass of whiskey. She was about to note that he was drinking too much alcohol but then stopped herself as she knew Bill wouldn't have liked her to say it. She cannot recall whether she brought the basket or whether she took the pills out and presented them to him on a plate. She might have said, but she is not sure, that she thought he had already taken his pills, but he said she was confused, and he knew what he was doing. She could hear the peremptory tone, the irritation in his voice. He was agitated, agitated by her. He might have even said that she was stupid, knew nothing. It wouldn't have been the first time he had said that. She remembers she apologised and then he did as well. Or did he? Sometimes, he would realise he had spoken to her too harshly. But maybe that time he didn't. No, she remembers thinking afterwards, days afterwards, that on that occasion he didn't apologise. A pity. His last chance. But he didn't know it. Nor did she. How could anyone have known it? While she was filling up the dishwasher, she heard a thump and a sound, a strange sound, maybe a sigh or a sharp cry. She didn't pay attention to any of it. Why not? Why didn't she go to check what it was? She felt hurt, hurt by his words. She knew nothing. That's what he told her. For the umpteenth time. She knew nothing. He didn't need her since she knew nothing. What was the point of finding out what had happened? She knew nothing. She walked to her study through the hall without casting a glance into the lounge. She rang Patricia to speak to her since the next day she and Bill were flying to New York, and she wanted to have a good chat with her best friend. She had told Patricia that she might be busy with packing but that she would try to ring her. But perhaps it was Patricia who rang her. Yes, it was Patricia but they had arranged the specific time and that's why she was in the study waiting for the call. By the time she returned to the lounge, she could see Bill was dead. She went to her room and tried to collect her thoughts. There was no rush to call anyone. It was too late. How come she knew he was dead? She just knew as she looked at him. He was lying on the floor. Or was it because she knew he had taken all those pills and he had to be dead? She didn't call the ambulance because she was shocked. And angry. She was angry for the years of him speaking to her harshly, as if she had been some kind of irritant, an imposition, a nuisance in his life. She needed time to pull herself together. She didn't say that to the police. But there was nothing that could have been done. It would have made no difference had she rung straight away. Had she told them that she needed time to collect herself, they might have asked more questions. The coroner wrote accidental death. Accident of death. Deadly accident. Overdose. They didn't say it was suicide. Maybe just an error. Whose error? Did she give him too many pills?

She wasn't around for the death of her parents. No one was there except those who died with them. A plane crash in Ireland. Big news it was. Not many people flew in those days, straight after the war. She had never been on a plane. No bodies were recovered. A few possessions of other passengers were beached months later and returned to relatives. Nothing of theirs was found. They would have died, lost consciousness before the plane, or their bodies, hit the water. That's what she was told. But they might have known what was happening, even if for a few seconds. She has often thought about that. What would have been on their mind? Their only child, a postgraduate at Oxford. Would they have prayed? She had lost her faith by then, but she held a mass for them. A priest from their church contacted her and it was his idea. Strangely, she hadn't thought of it. And she was glad she could do something they would have liked. She felt guilty, responsible for their death. No relatives, none whatsoever. Later, when she met Bill, he couldn't believe it when she told him. 'Not even distant cousins,' he asked. None that she knew of. There could not be many people with no relatives at all. At the mass, she hardly knew anyone. Members of the congregation, and a few people from her parents' respective places of work. Her father's choir sang. She was calm and felt strangely detached, still unable to comprehend that was it, that she was an orphan, that she was no longer anyone's child, that she was on her own in the world. But she broke down towards the end, as Faure's 'Requiem' was played. She had chosen it because it was music that could lift you off the earth towards heaven, taking you to the place she no longer believed in. She realised her tears were for herself, for the guilt she felt for the death of her parents, not for them. That was hard to cope with. Later she felt guilty about feeling guilty. How could she ever admit that to anyone? The priest asked whether she wished to speak to him, whether she needed confession. When she said no, she could see that he had assumed she attended church in Oxford. She didn't say anything.

In Oxford, a letter was waiting for her. She had been awarded a scholarship for a year of study in Paris. She remembers thinking that perhaps she wasn't responsible for the death of her parents after all. Perhaps someone up there was looking after her. Many years later she remembers mentioning that thought to Patricia and how Patricia had laughed. 'Once a Catholic, always a Catholic,' she said. 'That bloody guilt and shame have followed you.' There was something in it. She could never shake off her guilt for the death of her parents and then later, Guillaume. If only she could have stayed with her parents and their faith. How often she used to wish that. What was it that took her away from them? She had a happy childhood, even with the war on. Yes, there were shelters and not much food but most of the time, they stayed in Sussex, in a house her parents rented from a farmer whose sons were on the front and who had moved in with his sister. She remembers the three of them, her, a teenager sitting between her parents on the sofa, all quietly reading their books. She loved that magical silence when all you could hear was the gentle turning of a page, surrounded by the two people she loved, yet, the story in her lap allowed her to talk to others, without having to put up with their teasing and silliness, as happened at school. They teased her a lot at school. She still remembers they teased her for talking about books. She didn't understand why. Her evenings were spent reading or listening to classical music. Once a week, her parents hosted a musical evening and even when there were no visitors, her father played the piano and her mother sang. She was encouraged to join in. They were older than the parents of her friends - another reason for her classmates to mock her: why do you live with grandpa and grandma? - and she was aware that their household was different. She remembers she had loved the way they lived. She was proud of being different. She didn't remember ever being unhappy as a child and although an outsider might have seen her as lonely, that was not the case. Her parents were warm and affectionate with each other and towards her. She couldn't imagine leaving the house without a hug and a kiss. She remembers growing up talking about books and music, just like her school friends talked about dresses and boys. She valued her parents' opinions and there was no one else she admired as much as the two of them. But then it all changed. Overnight. Overnight, when she was thirteen and was confirmed and then, she remembers, within days of the celebrations, she discovered her clitoris – without knowing what it was, let alone what it was called – and started touching herself. Patricia thought it was neat and appropriate for the two things to go together. She remembers being puzzled. How confirmation and clitoris go together? 'Confirmation and discovering the clitoris, both signify coming of age, the entry into the adult world, the entry of the soul and the entry of the body. You did it by the book,' Patricia said. But she remembers not being able to see the funny side of it. In her mind, the secret sensations – usually in the bathroom, where she could lock the door without arousing her mother's suspicion – were inextricably linked to shame and guilt. She knew she was doing something forbidden, something she could not tell her parents, and that secret created a rupture. Until then, they were close. She remembers thinking of her parents as her best friends, her mother in particular. And then, it all broke down. She felt she had cut herself off: she rejected their hugs and kisses. And since she had no friends to speak to, discovering her sexuality meant being pushed into the world of loneliness for the first time in her life. She remembers that time when she ran into an old classmate in the theatre, many years into her marriage, and how strange it was that they recognised each other after all that time. The woman told her that the class used to call her Miss Prism, or was it Miss Prim? One or the other, and also Miss Goody Goody. They laughed at her behind her back imagining her playing the piano for hours on end and thought she would turn into an ageing spinster. The woman said how surprised they were when they realised that she was one of the first to get married.

She remembers how she used to own up to her private pleasure at confession and was given due penitence, yes, she remembers, that was to start with but after a while, she couldn't bear the priest's sanctimonious tone. She lied. By the age of fifteen, she was sufficiently independent-minded. How wonderful that she felt like that even at the time before reading de Beauvoir, yes, she was sufficiently independent minded to think that her body was her own. She persuaded herself that what she did to it was no one's business. There wouldn't have been anything she would have read to make her think like that. How advanced she was despite all the Catholic doctrine, how advanced and yet, and yet, she didn't develop in that vein. Not for a long time. What happened? Was it the marriage that stymied her? No, no, no. She mustn't blame Bill. She was happy. Or so she thought at the time. How come she has never asked that question before? She remembers the moment the priest asked her whether she had done anything dirty, yes, after a while he started asking her. Patricia said he was a dirty old man getting kicks out of listening to her confession. 'Probably touching himself at the same time,' Patricia added. Such an idea never crossed her mind and, anyway, he was not old. As for dirty, that was just a word. What was dirty? Patricia would have been the last one to call sex dirty. Why did she say that then? A shorthand, a shorthand we all use. She remembers when for the first time she had answered in the negative, no she hasn't been touching herself, and even though she said it without hesitation, he had repeated the question, as if he had sensed her uncertainty, she remembers feeling her throat tighten and she swallowed hard and said loud and clear: 'Yes, father. I am sure.' She remembers the apprehension when she walked home, how she feared retribution, taking extra care in crossing the road and not walking under scaffolding. But when nothing happened, the next time lying was easier, and after a while, she stopped thinking of her lies as lies.

But the shame stayed, and it grew worse. She remembers when she was a lanky seventeen-year-old, she allowed boys to walk her home; they would stop in a dark alleyway close to her parents' house, an ideal place for snogging. She always had one eye open, looking out for her father on his way home from choir practice or for one of the neighbours, returning from the pub. She would have died of shame if anyone had seen her with a boy's hand inside her bra. Not that her father would have said anything. But his stare over the breakfast table the following morning would have shamed her more than any words. When her parents were killed, she knew rationally it had nothing to do with her deception and that it would have been much worse had they died knowing she had sinned so badly. Besides, God would have been more than a little unfair on the other passengers: That's a funny thought; they couldn't all have had daughters submitting to their carnal impulses. But she couldn't shake it off. Her guilt remained. And more was to come. After Paris, she swore she would abstain for ever, curb her carnal desires, otherwise she might depopulate the world with her sins. What rubbish it all was. It took her a lifetime, and an extraordinary long lifetime it has been, to free herself from guilt. Did it damage her? How could one know? Anything we are brought up with can be damaging. You can always put it like that. Or the other way around. Anything that is lacking from our upbringing can be damaging. What was lacking, whatever it was, did it damage her? A pointless question. She is as she is and there is no way tracing the origins of what she is like. These days she feels no shame. Only love and contentment. She is happy.

She is looking forward to Martin's party. The staff would have held one yesterday for the other residents, with balloons and singing. She remembers seeing pictures from previous years. Martin doesn't like those parties, but he goes along with them. 'To be nice to the others,' he says. 'Not much else happens here.' Some of his fellow residents wouldn't know what's going on, but others enjoy the event. It is something to break up their monotonous lives. Today is a private party: Martin's old editor, only some ten years younger than him, and the literary executor will be there, also a representative from the publishers. Zach and Gabriel will come with her. The three of them are the family. Martin's only family. Like her, he was an only child. There will be no friends. Few people of his age have friends. At one hundred and two, there are only dead friends. Memories of friendships. She remembers reading somewhere a writer saying that personally he had nothing against ghosts since his best friends were dead. Spot on, she thought. But Martin was never a person who cultivated friends. Bill was his only friend, but that ended badly. They kept the friendship, she and Martin. A few ups and downs. He was stubborn, entertaining expectations about her once Bill was dead. She has loved him as a friend but there was something completely asexual about him. She couldn't imagine kissing him, let alone anything more intimate. He is not the only man she has found like that. Asexual. Nick had that about him, too. She admired him, he was kind, or rather kind to a point until she made it clear there was no hope for him. And then he turned difficult. It used to happen to Patricia, she remembers. A man professing undying love to her, saying she was his best friend and he loved her, and then when she told him she didn't feel like sleeping with him anymore, he would turn difficult, sometimes even nasty. 'It showed a man's true character,' Patricia would say. Only a man who doesn't value you as a person, who thinks of you as no more than a sexual object, would behave like that. That was her experience with Nick. She wished she could have been attracted to him but she couldn't force attraction. It is either there or it isn't. One needs to connect to another person as a thinking being, but also in the physical, visceral sense and, with Nick, the latter didn't exist. She couldn't fake it. She realised the importance of physical attraction which, at least in her case, has nothing to do with any conventional notion of beauty.

She remembers the man at the concert. Sometimes she wondered whether with someone like him it could have worked even if they didn't have any intellectual interests in common, even if he had been a builder. But no, she has always been a snob. She is not proud of that but at least she can claim points for self-knowledge. But if there is no visceral attraction, even no attraction of any kind, sex may work once, or twice possibly, with a story and role play. That's how it was with the masseur. He was right to make it clear it was a one off. No repeats. No repeat prescriptions. He must have known hardly anyone would find him attractive. He was one of the few she met through the dating agency. That was a 'wild Claire' thing, agreeing to meet him. Later, she wondered whether she had taken too much risk. She did give Patricia his details as well as leaving them prominently on the kitchen table at home but nevertheless, had he murdered her, all it would have meant is that the police could find him, which wouldn't have been much satisfaction to her. She remembers his piercing stare when he opened the door and asked her to sit down in a waiting room. A few minutes later, he called her from another room and asked her to come in. The lighting was subdued. The walls, doors and wooden shutters were painted in French grey. He had it all organised to a T. The soft, piano music reminded her of the atmosphere in a beauty salon; however, she was anything but relaxed. He told her to change into a gown behind the screen. He spoke with an officious tone. Didn't look at her. Fiddled with his papers. She was to remove everything except her underwear. He said he would get her notes. She remembers wondering what notes he was talking about and then she realised the reference acted as a prop, part of creating the atmosphere. Once behind the screen, she hesitated for a moment wondering whether she had taken too much risk. After all, they were in his flat, not in a public place, not even in a hotel room. What if he was Monsieur Landru? No, she was overreacting. She had checked him out. He was a retired senior lecturer in English at a second-rate university. Except that on the picture he looked different. But she was there and it would have been foolish to cry off. Foolish but it might mean staying alive, she remembers thinking. Or, dead and still foolish. No, she was being silly. She took off her clothes and placed them carefully on a chair. As soon as she slipped on the gown, she heard his footsteps. Had he been watching her? Was there a hidden camera? He shouted he was ready whenever Mrs Jones was. Her *nom de plume*. Or was it a *nom de guerre?* They were playing roles. That was arousing. It still turns her on. She hoped his role wasn't the one of a murderer. He would have been in his late sixties, a few years older than her, although the gold-rimmed specs and thinning, grey hair, combed to a side parting, made him look older. He reminded her of a pharmacist her father used to talk to when she was a child and whom she found forbidding. Even his clothes seemed to be from a previous era: a professional white coat over a dark shirt and an egg and bacon striped tie. He directed her to sit on the bed. A clipboard in one hand and a pen in the other, he stood in front of her. She remembers him saying that he had some idea of her problem from their telephone conversation but that he needed to complete a more detailed medical questionnaire. They had not spoken on the phone, but she understood it was part of the background to the roles they were playing. He checked through the list, asking about her health and she answered without giving it much thought. Was that really her? Almost thirty years have passed since and she remembers him, him and his voice, and those forbidding gold metal glasses but could she have really allowed herself to be in that situation? A mad Claire. As he went on, she didn't bother to answer truthfully. It was a game and making-up a story was part of the pleasure. He kept his eye on the notes and ticked the boxes and then he said he needed to examine her so that he could identify the source of the pain. He stood behind her and slipped his hands inside the gown. They were cold and smooth. When he pressed on her neck and as his hands moved down her back, he asked whether she felt pain. He applied pressure on particular spots. His thumbs prodded her vertebrae, slowly moving towards her bum. He rolled down the top of her knickers and held her buttocks, with his thumbs slipping in between. Yes, she remembers that touch, and she feels it now. Oh, yes. Slow and smooth. She hears his murmur. She was aroused, yes, she was. He scribbled a few notes, frowned, walked around the bed. Eventually he said, addressing her as Mrs Jones, that he had identified several points of extreme tension in her back. Without treatment, she was in danger of developing chronic migraines. He slipped on a pair of rubber gloves and picked up a bottle of oil from a trolley next to the bed. He worked his way over her neck and shoulders and it felt pleasant. By then she had forgotten about any fears. Arousal took over. That's all she felt. He said he was worried about the oil staining her bra and asked for permission to undo it. She remembers thinking that inch by inch, they would get there. And inch by inch was part of the arousal. A tantric method, she learned later. His hands thumped, circled and pressed on her back, moving up and down. It was the first time she'd a proper massage and it was as good as she could have imagined. Of course, Hal was miles better, but that was later, a few years later. No one could have been as good as Hal. She wondered whether the man was professionally trained. He carried on for a while and then asked her to lie on her back. He said he would like to examine her breasts. She stared at him, pretending to appear incredulous. She had grown into the role and he responded by saying it could provide some very useful secondary information but if she felt uncomfortable, she should tell him. He wouldn't like to cause discomfort, he said. She thought she should play the game and asked him if he really needed to. Delaying the inevitable turned her on. He said it wasn't strictly essential but that it would help enormously. She remembers that. All the time he addressed her as Mrs Jones. She sighed and then waited, as if she was trying to decide, before telling him to go ahead. She was lying on her back. Gently, he lifted off her bra and the fingers of both hands spread out like a fan and pressed on her breasts, the palms circled the aureoles. He pinched her nipples, harder and harder. She closed her eyes and held her breath. He apologised and said it was part of the examination. He ordered her to focus. And then? Then he sprinkled oil on her breasts and spent several minutes massaging them. His hands travelled to her shoulders and neck and then back to the chest. She remembers breathing slowly, holding her excitement in check. He asked if he was allowed to remove her knickers. She asked why and pretended to panic. Playing the role of a reluctant innocent, yes, that was an extra turn-on. He said it helped the treatment to be fully effective. He sounded irritated. She asked for further explanation. He said the main problem was in her pelvic bones. That was the source of her tension. He needed to check the muscles in the area. Any slight misalignment could have repercussions for everything else, her entire skeleton, her back. She said she wasn't sure. He said he would be gentle. And he was. And what did he do next? He removed the knickers, parted her legs and then his fingers started prodding inside her vagina, slithering oil over the clitoris and caressing the perineum. She kept her eyes closed but every now and then she opened them a fraction and she caught sight of his serious face. She could see no trace of excitement. He asked her to take deep breaths and relax. He could feel her tension, he said. It was important to excise all her anxiety. He placed a soft white towel over her eyes. It was an effort to take deep breaths as her excitement was growing and her breathing was racing. She was ready to be fucked. But he carried on examining and massaging her vagina, playing with the labia, ignoring her arousal. His telephone rang. He excused himself and asked her not to move a jot. She should stay as still as she could. She heard him walking away and remained motionless for what must have been five or ten minutes. When he came back, he looked at her and said he had asked her not to move. She said she hadn't. He said she was lying. She didn't understand the seriousness of the situation. The causes of her pain might be more widely spread than it appeared. He pulled the gown off her shoulders and his hands moved around her breasts, held them, pressed the flesh down, squeezed the nipples. Again, he repeated that it was important during this very delicate examination that she didn't move at all. His hands kneaded her breasts with greater strength and urgency than before. And then? What did he do then? He took a nipple in his mouth and sucked on it. A hand parted her legs, and a finger entered her. She uttered an involuntary sigh. He stopped immediately and stepped back. He shouted at her. His face was red with anger. He accused her of moving and wasting his time. Either she stayed still or she should get dressed and go. And no sound, he said. She had to concentrate. She promised. He said he couldn't take any more risk with this delicate examination. He blindfolded her, fixed her ankles onto hooks on the edge of the bed and tied her hands with straps, her arms spread wide open. 'Let's try for the last time,' he said to himself. She remembers she felt clips placed on the nipples. He massaged her breasts. He pushed a large blob of freezing cold jelly inside her and soon she was exploding with pleasure; her immobility increased her orgasm. He said he was pleased they completed this part successfully and could proceed with the rest. He removed the clasps and straps. And then? And then he unzipped his trousers and through a chink between her face and the cloth she could see as his erect penis popped out. His face kept its stern expression. He said they had to begin the treatment in earnest. She asked what he meant. He said she should keep quiet and follow his instructions. First, she needed to lift her bottom as high as she could. She obeyed. He climbed onto the bed and knelt behind her. Again, he addressed her as Mrs Jones. His tone was admonishing, she remembers. She had to relax, even if the next stage was uncomfortable, he told her. If she stayed tense, it would take much longer. He gripped her buttocks and without further ado pushed himself inside her. And then he proceeded to fuck her until she screamed and collapsed on the bed. He immediately pulled out, got off the bed and zipped his fly. She didn't think he ejaculated. He told her to get dressed. He said she should settle the bill with his secretary on the way out. He walked out and closed the door behind him. She waited for a few minutes but heard no sound. It was clear he wasn't coming back. She never saw him again. She knew her face was flushed as she walked to the tube. More than that, she remembers she didn't feel like herself. Was it because she couldn't shake off the role? Or was she too dazed by the orgasms? Blurry eyed? Probably. Just before she reached the station, she heard someone calling her name. Nick. That was unlucky. She was sure he could tell she wasn't herself. He asked her what she was doing in the area and she said she was visiting a friend. 'A physio, actually.' He asked whether she could recommend her. She remembers noting how he assumed the physio was a woman. He said something about his back problems. She made up a lie about the woman not taking new patients. She didn't think Nick believed her. That was the last time she saw him. A year later Marcel contacted her about the obituary. It was a heart attack.

She remembers giving a detailed account of the masseur to Patricia. How much she had changed by that time, how easy she found it to talk about sex. But it wasn't really sex as in making love. That's why she could disclose it. She wouldn't have talked about her and Hal. No, not in detail. That was too intimate, that was theirs; it wasn't hers to share with someone else. But the masseur, that was an elaborate game. Patricia thought that the guy would have masturbated afterwards. He would have got his kicks from exciting women, making them come. Above all, Patricia thought, it was about his control of women. His control throughout and then his control of his arousal, Patricia thought. That's why once he left the treatment room, he didn't reappear. He had to stop it there. He didn't want to be seen as excited, as someone who had lost control. He had power over women and that would have been his turn on. He had made it clear that he would only meet her once and that no matter how much she wanted to see him again, it would not be possible. Perhaps, it worked only once for him. He intrigued her, the way he used a common female fantasy of having to abandon herself to sex because it was absolutely necessary, and he did all that so that he could arouse himself. But it was pointless to rationalise his behaviour. By that time, she had learned that sexuality was a murky area that worked with its own, often unknowable parameters. The memory of the visit still excites her and sometimes she reaches for the vibrator. At other times, she wonders whether it had really happened like that or whether she had, over the years, embellished it with details from her own fantasies. It was so long ago and she is right to be suspicious of her recollection. Maybe it was all her fantasy. Not all. Maybe some of it, most of it. She couldn't have remembered all those details. These days, her sex life is nothing but fantasy. Fantasy and memories. Memories of fantasies. Or is it fantasies of memories? The memory of the masseur sends a buzz through her body. She has made use of it many times. But with Hal it is different. It is, yes, it still is, yes, all these years after his death, it still is. She can look into his face and she can talk to him. She hears him talk to her. She remembers the words he would say at the moment of his orgasm. She remembers the look on his face, the knot of lines around the mouth, the grip of his hands on her shoulders. The smell of his mouth. And she wishes they could have died together. She wishes that each time she thinks of him. But no, that's a romantic thought and a destructive thought. She loves her life now. She loves her memories. She recalls hearing an old person say many years ago – or perhaps it was a character in a novel – say that all they have are memories and that they have reached the age at which it is time to figure out what those memories mean. But what does anything mean? Whatever you want it to mean. Looking for a meaning in one's memories is a simplistic, but perhaps a comforting attitude to think that our lives have a meaning, let alone our memories.

She loves Zach. And Gabriel. Will there be time for Zach to read 'Prufrock' to her when he arrives? She longs to hear it. Prufrock, an old man with his trousers rolled up and measuring his life in coffee spoons. These images always come to her. Now, he is young. The age of Zach, no, younger, Prufrock is even younger than her son. Yes, she will be ready and, before they leave, they can sit down, and Zach will read to her.

She was sorry to have hurt Martin that day after the concert, and she is still sorry; how silly to be sorry after so many years but yes, she is. Does he still remember it? What does one remember at one hundred and two? Old grudges? Old flames? He rarely went out even in those days and she remembers she was pleased he joined her at the concert, what was it, was it Bach? Yes, it was a string quartet, yes, she was pleased he joined her but he shouldn't have entertained unwarranted expectations. Always unwarranted. But sometimes, just sometimes it crossed her mind whether she might have given him hope, unwittingly, by being friendly and open, at ease in his company. Or perhaps he started to entertain hopes in the days after Bill's death when she was too absorbed in what happened in her life and she had not noticed his attention. She was sorry to have hurt Martin, but she had to speak to the man at the concert. She had to tell him she wanted to see him again. And then when she realised that she had given him the wrong telephone number, a non-existent telephone number, she had to act. What a cunning plan it was. So unlike her, yes, that's what Patricia said. How did she think of it? Do people devise such schemes or does it happen only in novels? She couldn't tell whether it would work or whether she would embarrass herself in a spectacular fashion, but she had to take the risk. In fact, she felt so strongly about seeing the man that she thought she had no choice but to act. She rang the venue at St Martin's and told them that she and her husband, and yes, she stressed that she was there with her husband, had talked to a couple sitting next to them at a recent Vivaldi concert and, accidentally, they had taken away a book that the people had shown them. Now they felt guilty but didn't know how to return it. But was it a Vivaldi concert? Martin wasn't a fan. Bach, yes, Bach was his kind of music. And hers. But perhaps it was Vivaldi. Perhaps he would have gone with her because in those days he still entertained his hopes. That's why he would have come with her even if it was Vivaldi. Anyway, she asked the woman at the box office whether the venue could ring the people sitting next to them and ask them to get in touch with her or with her husband and she kept apologising and the woman in the box office said she wasn't allowed to reveal customer's details but she was happy to ring them and then it was up to them whether they wished to proceed. She also said that she could only trace the other customers if they had booked on the phone and paid by card, and then she checked and yes, that was the case and so she promised that she would ring them. The woman was very sympathetic and didn't doubt her story at all. How grateful she was to the woman in years to come. Grateful for helping her and grateful for not being suspicious, grateful for trusting her fib. And she recalls feeling a strange exhilaration at inventing the story, at being daring, which was so unlike her usual self. Oh, how she enjoyed her little deceit. And the plot bore fruit. But she was lucky that the call came during her lesson and she didn't answer it. For it was the man's wife who had rung and left a message, saying that she had a call from the box office at St Martin's and adding she didn't understand what it was about a book that they mentioned. She remembers the excitement and fear she felt after she had listened to the message. Now she had the number and she rang it but there was no response. Only an answerphone, stating that it was the household of Rebecca and Hal but that they were not available. She didn't leave a message. She remembers feeling pleased to know his name. As if that would have helped. As if she could have looked for and found Hal, found Hal in London, Hal who lived with Rebecca. Knowing the number, she could take another chance. And she did. And she was lucky. The man, the man from the concert, the man with that extraordinary face, answered. For years after that, for years she could look at his face and feel the joy, the pleasure of her orgasm. That word, the word she never liked the sound of, that word that sounds so technical. Is it technical to say orgasm? It always makes her think of construction work, work on a building site with lots of metal beams. Crude certainly. But *jouissance. Jouissance.* Yes. Why the French always do it better? *Jouissance.* She was silly thinking like that, Patricia said, and she had to agree and then she remembered there is *orgasme* in French too, not to mention that *jouissance* is also a word lawyers use. And then Patricia asked her whether she had slept with a French lawyer and they both laughed since they both knew, Patricia through her business dealings in France, that *jouissance* was a word in legal documents. They could be silly, the two of them. She still misses Patricia, thirty years later. But Hal. The ruggedness of his face. Did he remind her of Leonard Cohen? Not then. No, but later, later yes, the two merged in her mind. Looking at his face was even lovelier than kissing him. No, no that couldn't have been true.

What she would give to see that face again. But what could she give? Years of her life? Yes, if she had any.

❧

Nick left her cold. There was nothing either of them could do about it. She wanted it to work out. He was an attractive man in an obvious, conventional way. He was a Francophile, fluent in French, a great pâtissier. All of that was in his favour, she kept telling herself, she remembers. Later, when he came out in his true colours and his kindness was shown to be fake, she was glad it hadn't worked out. But was it really fake? Was she being unfair? For he was hurt, and when people are hurt they find it hard to be kind. But perhaps they were his true colours. Patricia said the same and told her of her first boyfriend, a would-be poet, who insisted on giving her a typed up, stapled collection of his writing but when they split up, or rather, when she left him, he insisted she returned it to him and wouldn't wait for her to find the time to do it. Patricia thought it was a good test to check what kind of man she was dealing with. Tell them it's all over and see how they react. Suddenly all those protestations of love evaporate and morph into toxic behaviour. But with a good person, their love still shows, she said. Nick wasn't a good person, she remembers thinking at the time. When it comes to the crunch, one shows one's true colours. And his true colours were ugly. It all started with a present, the present Bill had bought her for her fiftieth birthday: a pâtisserie course run by a well-known Parisian chef. She had loved baking but nevertheless the choice of the present surprised her since Bill was not a cake eater. Even in good restaurants, he would not order a dessert. A man with no sweet tooth; that was disconcerting. She remembered then and she remembered all through her life, the medical student at a friend's party when she was fifteen, and that twenty-year old student was the only man at the party. He seemed clever and amiable, and so much older, and all the girls gathered around him and took his words as truth. That man had said that they should look for a boyfriend in a pâtisserie because men who liked cakes were more emotional and that characteristic, in the mind of the man, was a good thing, a good thing for a boyfriend. He might have even said that men who liked cakes were more caring. She had laughed at that and she didn't take it seriously, but it had stayed with her and resurfaced when Bill came into her life. She knew it was silly, but perhaps not as silly as the belief of a teenage friend who claimed that if people didn't have straight legs, they couldn't be trusted. Sooner or later they would betray you. She had laughed at the friend, but the friend assured her that she had numerous examples to prove the veracity of her claim. We all have our little whims, sometimes more than whims. Martin always says he greatly distrusts people with religious faith. But is that a whim? It sounds more rational than cakes and legs.

Bill loved when she baked. He said it created a warm atmosphere in the house. The smell of cinnamon. Or lemon, she remembers him saying. The day after he had told her of the present, he added that he had always been proud of her whenever they had dinner guests and how he loved when they commented on her cakes, wondering whether she had bought them from a special pâtisserie, and once she had done the course, he said, she would be able to dazzle them even more. That's what Bill said, she remembers. That was fine, she thought, it gave her pleasure to please him, it gave her pleasure to please his friends, but she would have preferred he had not put it like that. She was not some trophy wife. But she had enjoyed baking, still does, so there was no point complaining. Besides, Bill loved her and even if she was impersonating a wife, a trophy wife, that was fine. Impersonating a wife. That thought never crossed her mind when she was a wife. It came much later. She remembers once reading a story about a lonely woman who baked huge quantities of cakes in the hope that someone would eat them, and love her, but she ended up giving all of them to the ducks in the park. 'Baking for love', yes, that was the story's title. At fifty, she had identified with the woman in that story: she too baked to be loved, loved by Bill, loved properly. Loved more than being 'his dear, little Claire'.

The pâtisserie course was an exciting present but as soon as she had booked accommodation, a studio flat in the Marais, Bill had his stroke. She cancelled the trip, hoping to go once he recovered. He did, but then it wasn't convenient, and she postponed again. Later she was too bereft to face going to Paris and booked a pâtisserie course at a local college. She remembers enrolling on the course out of loyalty to her dead husband, a misplaced loyalty, according to Patricia. 'What's the point,' Patricia said, 'Bill wouldn't know you are doing the course. He's dead.' But she was doing it for herself. Patricia said she was being absurd and laughed at her, telling her how she would be surrounded by old grannies baking buns and asked whether she was planning taking up knitting. How funny that sounds now. If only Patricia were around. Would she still be dating? She too had expected lots of old women and was surprised when the rest of the class arrived. She was by far the oldest among the group of loud, giggly, yummy mummies who treated the Saturday morning purely as a social occasion. None of them seemed interested in the refined French pâtisserie that was described in the course brochure. All they wanted was to learn to bake themed, birthday cakes for their little darlings. She remembers being impressed at the sangfroid Nick had shown in the face of their expectations and how quickly he managed to accommodate their requests. She was amused by the way the sessions became a theatre of flirtation. They would stand much too close to him, flashing their blindingly white smiles, or bend down to retrieve a baking mould right in front of him, their substantial cleavages bobbing up and down, or they would suggestively lick the cake mixture through puckered lips, à la Nigella. Nick didn't seem to notice; he certainly didn't respond.

She was the only one who took his teaching seriously and she felt out of place. At the first session, fifteen minutes before the end, while Nick was halfway through a demonstration on how to use a piping bag, the women started to leave, each one with the excuse of having to collect their child from football, a piano or drama class. She and Nick were left alone surrounded by a pile of dishes and half used packets of flour, sugar and raisins spilling over the worktops. She remembers having theatre tickets for a matinee and she was anxious as she wanted to go home and change. But she felt guilty and thought it would have been rude to disappear without offering to help. While she was thinking what to do, Nick asked if she could do him a favour and help him clear up. The personnel officer was waiting for him and she had to leave soon. They started working from opposite ends and then the personnel officer walked in and asked Nick if he was ready to come to the office. He looked at her and she felt she had no choice but to say she would look after the tidying up. She emptied out the dishes, stacked them into the dishwasher and put away the left-over ingredients. When all was done, she wiped the surfaces, rinsed the cloths and gathered her bags. She was ready to rush off when Nick appeared, thanked her and invited her for a coffee. She remembers she was glad she could decline without having to invent an excuse. She remembers finding something about him disconcerting. Yes, from the start. Perhaps it was the hint of a French accent, which, in the past, she would have found attractive, but his was clearly affected. Was it meant to boost his credibility as a pâtisserie chef, she wondered? From his bio in the course brochure, she knew he was English but had spent several years living in France, working for well-known pâtissiers. The scene after the first session was repeated each week for the next three months. The women were loud and flirtatious and he remained immune to their displays. They disappeared in a hurry before the class finished and she stayed to help him tidy up. Each time he suggested a coffee in the canteen and each time she made an excuse. On the very last day, she accepted and even then, she wondered what Bill, only six months dead, would have thought if he could have seen her happily chatting with another man. She remembers she couldn't relax. She weighed every single word and she felt Bill watching over her shoulder.

A week after the course had finished, she received a small packet with two boxes, each containing six macarons, two red, two green and two brown. The box carried the name of *Le Macaron Rose*, and an address in East London. A note from Nick thanked her for helping him on the course. He said he would be delighted to show her around his kitchen and café. Could she let him know when it would be convenient for her? She replied by card, thanking him for the macarons but made no reference to his invitation. She remembers a few months later, he rang her to ask a favour. He said his staff had accepted an order to bake a cake for a celebrity party, he mentioned the name of some ex-football player, and the request involved making a cake inspired by Monet's paintings of waterlilies. He wasn't happy about baking that kind of cake, but he felt they had to honour the order. He was aware that she was knowledgeable about art and he wondered whether she could help and introduce him to Monet, look at the paintings with him? At first, she was flattered but then realised it was just the ruse: what was there to know about Monet to help you bake a cake? And, she has to admit, the flattery was welcome, even though she felt she could never get close to Nick. There was something essentially impenetrable about him. Yes, that's what it was. He was an archetypal single man, a man who didn't need anyone close, a man who was emotionally self-sufficient.

❧

Perhaps something about Nick reminded her of Bill, his detachment, his air of impenetrability, and she was wary. She is not sure she made the comparison at the time. Rather, it was her instinctive wariness. It took her years to realise that there was a fine line between not feeling needy and being self-sufficient. There were men who were too clingy and scared her off and there were men like Nick and Bill, men who asserted their emotional independence and made her feel superfluous. No, it's unfair to say she felt superfluous living with Bill. She had her role, and a big role it was. But it was a supportive role; her role was to make sure Bill could carry on with his work without being bothered by the stress of everyday life. Sometimes she thinks, but perhaps that's unkind, unkind to Bill and unfair, and she knows she didn't feel like that during her marriage, but sometimes it occurs to her she was his housekeeper, a lover and a friend, but not a close friend, not a confidante. She remembers Martin once saying something similar but then she didn't take him seriously. She thought Martin was jealous of her dead husband. She remembers it was something to do with following Bill's rituals and Martin being angry, saying that she was living too much in the past. Ridiculous of him to say that when he had remained engaged to his dead fiancé for the rest of his life. But she kept that to herself. It was true that Bill was one of those people who didn't need a confidante. All he needed was someone to look after the mundane side of his life. Someone to take care of the things he didn't think he should deal with because he wasn't prepared to spend time on the trivia of daily life. He kept his energy for his work. And he did acknowledge her contribution, in public, repeatedly. 'Without my dear, little Claire, I would not have had the time for my research and would have achieved much less. I owe her a lot.' That was nice but later, many years later, after his death, it crossed her mind that Bill had forced her in that role, his housekeeper and occasional lover. And yes, she had been happy. Very happy. At least that's what she thought at the time. But later she was resentful. She should have been asked, she should have been allowed to make her choice. She would have imagined that other couples discuss who will do what once they start living together. She recalls Patricia saying that at the time but she dismissed her friend's advice. How could she have taken her seriously, particularly when Patricia suggested that she should consider taking an occasional lover? Patricia wasn't being fair and she told her off. But perhaps Patricia had a point when she said that an occasional lover would rejuvenate her, make her feel valued and generally bring a breath of fresh air to her marriage. But she never considered it seriously.

Bill always wanted to make love on Saturday night. It was their regular slot. She didn't mind the regularity but later, after she had been through the experience with Jon and a few others, she wondered why his desire always resurfaced at that particular time, once a week? Is she being unkind if she thinks it was less a desire but just a need, a biological need? And what about her? Did it ever cross his mind to wonder on which day her desire resurfaced? If only she had known how to say it, how to say it then.

She used to think that Martin was like Bill because he lived his life alone, appearing emotionally self-sufficient. While Bill and he were good friends, for over thirty years, they were not what she would call intimate friends. She is no longer sure whether it was Martin who spoke to her about Bill needing her to be his housekeeper or whether the idea was sparked when she read one of Martin's novels. She remembers when she was helping him move to the sheltered accommodation, ten years ago it must have been, he pointed out one of his novels – she has had her own copies of all of them – and he said that the story might interest her. When she read it, she realised it might have been the novel that precipitated the quarrel between Martin and her husband. Or perhaps it was the other one, the one with Dr Williams, a married man who made regular visits to those Christelles and what were the others, yes, Annabelles. In one of those two novels, the main character is a middle-aged man whose wife killed herself after their first child had been born with severe disabilities and had died a few months old. He was committed to his work and, finding himself alone, he realised he needed someone to make sure that he could function without having to spend time on organising cooking and cleaning. He needed a wife, preferably a young wife, not set in her ways, a wife who would take care of his daily requirements but whose character and youth would also allow him to be a kind of parent, someone who guided her and helped her develop. He didn't want any children; the experience from his first marriage had been too traumatic. The character was on the lookout for a young, pliable woman to become his partner. Soon after he found such a woman, they started living together and she became pregnant. It was an accident he had tried to avoid and pleaded with her to have an abortion. He threatened to leave her. Before she died, apparently by her own hand, she had sent a letter to her family and to the police warning them that the man was threatening to poison her with pills and that he would present it as suicide. The novel starts with the arrest of the man. He is charged with the murder of his second wife and the police reopen the investigation into the death of the first one. Both women had killed themselves by taking pills that he, a research pharmacist, would have been able to obtain. The case against him seems overwhelming. She remembers that the idea of a character who had uncontrolled access to all kind of pills, as indeed Bill did, and who took them home, made her think of something Bill told her about Martin. It was one of those occasions when the two had a disagreement over a minor issue, and Bill was upset and said that one had to be careful letting a writer into one's life and home. 'You never know what they might use in their next book,' Bill said. It took him years of being Martin's friend before he realised he should be wary. 'Martin was like Big Brother,' he said. 'Wanting to know everything about you. Being a writer didn't give him licence to pry and steal.' She read the novel Martin had mentioned might be relevant to her, but she didn't talk to Martin about it. What would have been the point? To get confirmation of Bill's secret life? The life of visiting Annabelless and Christells? Or if it was the other story, it would have only upset her to talk about Martin's vision of her marriage, of Bill marrying her only because he needed a housekeeper. In any case, by the time she had flicked through the novel, Bill had been dead for more than twenty years. She had no interest in knowing things that no longer mattered, just as she wasn't interested in scoring points when Bill was alive. She remembers Martin once said, when he was annoyed with her for behaving, as he put it, like a Greek village widow and living only for Bill's memory, Martin said that Bill was an obsessive and controlling person who needed her more than she needed him. That was uncalled for. It hurt her and she told him so. He must never again say anything like that about Bill. And he didn't. He apologised. What did it matter who needed whom more? And it was unfair to say that Bill couldn't afford emotions, or that he feared them. It was not true. Sometimes it seems to her that they were both running away from something. They were running away from whatever frightened them. But couldn't one say that about everyone? Running away from or running towards something. And always waiting.

She once heard someone say that the whole world is one large waiting room. We are forever waiting for something to happen or someone to arrive. What's she waiting for now? Zach, she is waiting for Zach. She is waiting for the party. No, she is not waiting for death. Her life's too good.

They were happy together, she and Bill. They were happy because she didn't allow herself to think otherwise. But she is happy now. She is happier now, happier than ever.

When the two men first met, Bill was a medical student and Martin a precocious teenager, not yet a published writer. Bill said that Martin was training himself to think like a writer and, for a writer, everything he sees in another person can be useful, for characterisation, for a story. He never stopped gathering information. 'I should have taken note of that then,' Bill said. 'I should've have been wary of him.' One thing Martin particularly enjoyed, Bill told her, was when visiting someone in their home was to go to the bathroom and open the cabinet. According to Bill, Martin did it throughout his life. Unfailingly, Bill claimed Martin had told him, the inside was a revelation: rows of medication and personal grooming items that were a treasure house of possible stories. What kind of deodorant they used, what kind of toothpaste, interdental brushes, creams, ointments. And the pills? The pills were a mine of stories. Bill said there should be a law where a writer would be obliged to present a government warning to anyone they met. 'We should make sure that people are aware of the potential danger of letting a writer into their lives,' Bill would say. She remembers thinking he was being paranoid. For him, a story mattered only if it was true, by which he meant it happened. In real life, as he used to say. She tried to point out that once a story was in a novel, it was fictional, no matter how close to real life it was. Bill's reading approach, she thought, wasn't much different from those people pronouncing fatwas because they allege a work of fiction had insulted their religion. They too couldn't tell that a novel is a fictional text.

Martin didn't ask her whether she had read the novels he had suggested might be of special interest to her. Perhaps he was waiting for her to mention them. Or perhaps he had forgotten about them in the mêlée surrounding his move to the home. But there was nothing to talk about. She had been aware of Bill's first marriage and the death of his baby daughter or, was it a son? He had told her about his life before they were married and he had said he would prefer if she were never to raise it as it was too painful for him. She understood. The rest didn't matter. The Annabelles, no, they were irrelevant. She had a happy marriage. Yes, that's what she kept telling herself for many years. Even had that not been the case, what would have been the point of growing bitter about the past?

Martin's novel didn't tell her anything new. But she wondered why Bill hadn't told Martin that she knew about the tragedy of his first marriage. Probably, for the same reason that he had asked her not to mention it. Clearly, Martin had used Bill's life for the story, but it seemed to her disingenuous of him to suggest that Bill needed her to take on the role of a child and a housekeeper. But so what if he did? He was kind to her and she was happy. They were happy together. Or so she thought. Besides, when she met him, she was an orphan, a young woman still in need of parents, she believed, and, in some ways, he did fill that role. Why would it have been wrong, then, if he saw her as his child?

The other day she heard a radio programme about *Le Macaron Rose*. They were celebrating their fiftieth birthday. The founder, Nick Swinton, had been dead for twenty years but the pâtisserie has continued to thrive. Its current owner, Marcel Gayet, who was trained by Nick, and took over upon Nick's death, was interviewed. He was asked about the name of the café and said that behind the name there was a moving story that Nick had written in his autobiography, which he had specified should be destroyed after his death, but Marcel said he had no heart to do it. He said it was a story that many people might learn from. The autobiography, *Le Macaron Rose*, was published as part of the celebrations marking the fifty years of the café and Marcel Gayet said he was sure that when people read it, they would agree that he had done the right thing to act as Max Brod to Nick's Kafka. She agreed with Marcel. If an author wanted something destroyed, they should do it themselves. Asking their executor to do it is disingenuous, she remembers thinking. It puts pressure on them and besides, it smacks of false modesty. It's saying, my work is really no good, but I don't want to destroy it. Why not? Because a *tincy wincey* part of me thinks that it is good but I haven't the guts to admit it. I will leave it to others, hoping they will disobey my instructions. After the interview, she remembers Marcel reading sections from the autobiography where Nick writes that, in his life, he had been luckier than most, professionally and privately. He had been married to Caroline, whom he called the most wonderful woman in his life, and they had a twelve-year old daughter, Alice. He was aware that it may sound as implausibly romantic when he said that nothing could have been better in their marriage. For two years, they ran a restaurant and worked hard to make it a success. They gained a Michelin star, but soon after Caroline started complaining of headaches. They attributed it to stress, the pressure of work. He assumed that when that eased off, her headaches would disappear. To his eternal regret, he did not insist on her having a check-up, assuming that she would be told the problem was to do with stress and she would be offered tranquillizers. He was forever to blame himself for not paying more attention to what was happening. Caroline had odd moments of confusion, forgetting names and dropping dishes in the kitchen. Often, she would be sick in the morning. There were days when her speech was slurred. Textbook symptoms of a brain tumour, but he ignored them. One morning she was driving Alice to school and she lost control of the car. The girl was killed instantly but Caroline lived for a few hours and died on the operating table. It was only then that they discovered her cancer, an aggressive type but it was still possible that, had she been diagnosed early, she might have been cured. She certainly wouldn't have been driving and Alice would not have been killed. Nick blamed himself. He would have given up anything, his life and all, if only he could have turned the clock back. He felt he had died with his wife and their daughter. She remembers feeling for Nick as she listened to Marcel reading from the book. It surprised her how she was overwhelmed by warmth for Nick. She wondered whether she could have loved him had she known the story at the time when she had first met him? But would it have been love, or a protective, nurturing, sympathy, borne out of sadness for the other and even more out of the misplaced belief that she could have made him happy? That she could have made him happy if only she had been more understanding, less self-centred, more attuned to his needs. But isn't that old Claire speaking, again, the Claire who spent her married life attuned to Bill's needs? Perhaps the reason for Nick's emotional detachment lay in the tragedy suffered by his family rather than a smug self-sufficiency. She must guard against such speculations, against what might have been. Nick managed to hold himself together for the funerals but afterwards nothing mattered any more. He abandoned the restaurant. He shut himself in the house, stopped eating and spent most of the time in bed, numb. All he could think was that he had killed them. Had he not been so obsessed with the success of the restaurant, he would have paid more attention and Caroline might have been treated in time. He was too ambitious, too greedy and he was taught a lesson. Now he had nothing. He didn't deserve to live. Eventually, he passed out. They had to break into the house to find him. He was hospitalised and stayed on a psychiatric ward for several months, before being moved to an asylum. He refused to see anyone. They had to feed him intravenously to keep him alive. A friend came twice a week and was desperate to get him out. He feared that Nick would die in that place which, he claimed, bore resemblance to the asylum in *One Flew Over a Cuckoo's Nest*, complete with a sadistic matron. The friend hired a psychiatrist, a Frenchman living in London, and this man spent many hours with the patient before Nick was allowed out into his care. For days, Nick refused to speak or even acknowledge the psychiatrist's presence. The psychiatrist took time to tell him his own story of a personal loss and of his recovery. As soon as the psychiatrist felt Nick was fit to travel, he organised for him to stay in a monastery in Nepal, the same place where the psychiatrist had lived for years. It was an ascetic establishment, high in the mountains. The monks worked in a tea plantation in a valley nearby. They lived in cells with earthen floors and ate simple, vegetarian fare. Nick mostly worked in the kitchen, helping in the plantation when he was needed. Weeks would pass without him exchanging a single word with anyone. People kept to themselves, doing whatever they were assigned to do. They all had their silent burdens. He had neither the need nor the desire to communicate. There was no radio or television, no phone, no post and he never wrote a single word. He lived in a constant present, with no future or past. He had no memories or plans. He existed, less like an animal, more like a plant, a mass of cells. Yes, those were the words Marcel Gayet read. And then the transformation.

One day, Nick was crossing the yard on the way down to the valley to pick tea, with a basket strapped to his back, keeping his eyes on the ground. A small hand came into his vision and said: 'Goûtez-un, monsieur.' A girl, no more than four years old, barred his way and he had to stop. 'C'est bon,' she said as she stretched her hand in front of him, holding a red macaron. He took it and stood there in the middle of the yard, in the baking sun, motionless. Later, months later, he wondered what had happened to her that day. He had not seen her go away. Eventually, he turned back and went into his room. He wrapped the biscuit in a piece of paper. After that, everything was a blur. He was ill for several days, hallucinating with fever. Monks came in with medicinal teas and held up his head, offering him sips. Once he recovered, he knew that his stay at the monastery had come to an end. The girl was a sign he had to obey. The fact that she spoke French and had brought him a macaron, another confectionery he associated with his tutor at Oxford, strengthened his belief that he had to start a new life at home. Hence *Le Macaron Rose*.

She will buy the book. But she knows the story of the Nepal monastery. Marcel was wrong when he said that Nick had never told the story to anyone. It would have been Nick's last shot with her. His last try. And it almost worked. She was moved when she heard it. But why didn't he tell her of the tragic deaths of his wife and daughter? What if, what if he had told her that? Don't go there, Claire, not again. Do not speculate. No, she has no regrets. She falls into speculation only to amuse herself. Yes. That's the reason. Yes, only to amuse herself with a story, a story that could have happened but didn't. A road not taken. A road? Roads, and roads. She could have loved him. But that would have been out of pity. Perhaps not. It would have allowed her to put his detachment in context, understand it. But anyway, what's wrong with a love out of sympathy? Is it not real love? What is real love? Was her love for Bill real? Or was it love out of gratitude? Stop, Claire. It was a happy marriage. She should stop saying that. There is no one she needs to convince.

But was it a happy marriage?

She remembers she ran into Nick in the cook shop in Richmond, a few years after the course. By that time, he seemed to have given up inviting her to *Le Macaron Rose.*

Was it last Saturday she saw reviews of Nick's autobiography? No wonder she has been thinking about him. But then, she thinks most days of the people she has known, let alone those she had loved, or who she might have loved. Hah. But she didn't love Nick. Nor did he love her. No. Had he really loved her, he would have accepted her friendship, he would have understood that she could not have given him more. Not sulking, being difficult, rude even. No, he didn't love her. Somehow their images, the memories of them . . . them? the men she cared about, the necessarily unreliable memories – she knows they are unreliable but that's all she has – swirl around her head, some of them for no more than a split second but the people live with her, alive or dead. She talks to Patricia every day and Patricia replies, she hears her laughter, her mockery, even her anger, and tears when yet another man failed her. The quick and the dead fill her days. Many more dead than quick. Sometimes she wonders what her parents might have thought of in those last few seconds between realising that they were about to die and losing consciousness. At her age, every day could be the last and it often occurs to her, when memories flood her brain, that perhaps her life is flashing in front of her eyes for the last time before she dies, a way of saying goodbye to all those people. A way of reliving her life in fast forward.

Nick's last try almost worked. She remembers going home and thinking how she had misjudged him and how he was not a cold, self-sufficient person, one of the Bill tribe. She might have misjudged him, but nevertheless there was the physical aspect. That was important. She realised that with Hal. By general standards, Nick was a very attractive man, exceptionally so, as Patricia kept reminding her, slim and well-spoken, with the face of a Hollywood actor. Oh, but she never found those beautiful, let alone attractive, and yes, Nick was successful, clever, a reader, an opera fan, yes, he was an opera fan, apparently. Well, that's what it said in his autobiography but he never mentioned it to her. How strange not to mention it to a musician. Why not, that could have been another trump card, another thing in his favour, but then, physically, sexually, he didn't have whatever it is that excited her. All the other men she had been with had it to some degree, but none more than Hal. Professor Henry Joseph M Labinsky. Her Hal. She remembers the thrill she felt the second time she rang his home number and he answered. They arranged to meet at lunchtime the next day on the South Bank. He was there before her, spotted her and walked towards her and she knew, she knew then, that second she saw him, she knew that she had never known anyone to whom she was as physically attracted as to him. She remained on high each time she saw him, every single time. He was married, of course he was, she knew that, she remembered the recorded message on their answerphone. His wife would have been one of the two women at the concert. He had thought she was married too and that Martin was her husband. Well, that wasn't such a silly assumption, but she laughed, thinking it ridiculous. She couldn't have been married to Martin. No, not at the time but had she met Martin when she had met Bill, that wouldn't have been so surprising, so silly. She had more in common with Martin than with Bill. But Martin wasn't pushy, not like Bill. Bill saw her and took the matter into his hands. In those days, doctors used to be like that. Authoritative. They behaved as if they knew everything. She disliked the attitude but when she met Bill she didn't think of that. She was lost, yes, his 'dear, little Claire'. No, she must stop thinking like that. Yes, doctors used to have authoritative manner, ordering everyone around, knowing everything. It isn't like that anymore and that's a good thing. But not writers, no. Had she met Martin when she was twenty, he would never have treated her in the way Bill did. Writers are tentative, the best ones are, uncertain. They are often shy and lacking in confidence. Like her.

At their first date, they kissed in public, she and Hal, a long, slow, gentle kiss, the best of her life. She can say that since, at ninety-two, there will be no more kisses to compare. The world around them ceased to exist. But it didn't. The world swirled, forever turning, making her feel dizzy. When she walked to the station, alone, she thought everything looked more beautiful than before. Yes, the world was a wonderful place. Hal illuminated everything. Her Hal. She remembers speaking to Patricia about the major obstacle: he was married. What pain might she create for another woman? She and Patricia had camped at Greenham in their youth, had attended anti-war demonstrations and had campaigned for the criminalisation of men who paid for sex. But feminism was also about female solidarity. Yes, Hal had said that he and his wife had not slept together for a long time, and he had had affairs throughout his life but . . . , and for her there was always that but. She knew that if women behaved as if they were rivals, competing for male attention, it was to the man's benefit. Patricia said what mattered was how truthful the man was about his situation and about how discreet the two of them were.

'Sometimes, it helps the marriage. As long as you remain cautious, it could be good for everyone.'

Good? No, it wasn't good. It was brilliant. Bloody brilliant. Perfect. Hal knew exactly how to touch her, Hal knew instinctively what excited her. It turned out they liked and disliked the same positions, the same movements. She shudders at the memory of how he would take out a little bottle, a little plastic bottle full of lubricator, and gently place some on her labia. He apologised for the cream being cold. But the chill, the touch of his fingers depositing the cold, sticky cream, that alone set her on the path to explosion. And he was a masseur for the gods. She would lie down on her front and he would sit astride her, his testicles tickling the space between her buttocks, and how aroused she would be by then, mad with excitement, shivering with anticipation of what was to come. He worked his hands across her back, gentle and strong until neither of them could resist anymore. He would enter her slowly. Very slowly. Each time she would have two, sometimes three, orgasms. She remembers thinking how wonderful it would be if the two of them were to die at that moment and by the time they were found, their bodies would be rigid, inseparable. In a story by Italo Calvino, a character dies sitting up; the only way they can bury him is by constructing a special coffin. They would have needed a special coffin to hold their forever united bodies, buried together.

Looking at his face was even lovelier than kissing him. Aaah, kissing him. Hal. Her Hal. Professor Henry Joseph M Labinsky.

Did she love him? She thinks she did but she didn't think about it at the time, she didn't think about it until years later. She was too overwhelmed by the physical attraction, by the power of their sexual encounters. Everything else was pushed into the background. Or perhaps she loved him in a way that she took for granted. No, he didn't take her for granted but she took her love for him for granted. It was there, always there. Sometimes she wondered, sometimes she wondered, what would have happened had he been single? Would they have lived together and, if so, would they have been able to maintain that intensity of attraction? He knew her body better than anyone else, he knew what her body needed, he knew what her body responded to better than she did. He knew all of that instinctively. He knew it the first time. He knew it because they were made for each other. But with that face he wouldn't have needed to do anything. She could just look into his face and have an orgasm, one that made her body weightless as though she was flying above the world, like one of Chagall's lovers or the woman in a novel she had read a long time ago, by some foreign writer, one of those autofiction texts, the woman who at sixteen had met an acrobat and flew with him above her town. What a lovely image. Orgasm as flying, much more appealing than orgasm as a little death. She remembers in the story the man was wearing tails and a top hat and the woman wondered how he managed to keep his top hat on despite the breeze. She liked that detail, that touching detail. She remembers that the woman spent the rest of her life sustained by the memory of that night flying above the town with her acrobat lover. Just as making love with Hal sustained her for the rest of her life. Each time she touches herself or takes out the vibrator, she thinks of Hal. She is with him. There would be no point thinking of anyone else. And she remembers that each time Hal was about to apply the lubricator on her labia – that thoughtful gesture, that caring gesture of a man who knows that a woman of certain age may be dry – and she remembers thinking at the time that even had the cream not been effective as a lubricator, it would have worked because it showed his kindness, and she has often found kindness from a man sexual. Kindness is a turn on, a bigger turn on than anything else. She wishes . . . she wishes . . . oh, for that moment now. If she could see Hal once more, just once, she would be ready to die and die happy. She wishes the world were ruled by the ancient Greek gods and she could make a pact with them, offer them anything they asked for in return for seeing Hal once again.

Yesterday, as she does most days, perhaps every day, yesterday she thought of his face but she found it difficult to see it in her mind's eye. She panicked and looked for the photograph that she had kept all these years, a photograph that she had enlarged to focus on his face. She couldn't find it on her iPad, and she was becoming anxious as she feared that she might have lost it and if she couldn't look at it, the memory of his face would gradually fade and she would not like to live the rest of her life without being able to recall that face, that beautiful face. She dropped everything else, didn't get dressed, stopped answering calls, she knew she couldn't do anything until she located the photo. She thought she would have to ask Zach to help her search and she even thought of ringing him to come straight away, but that would not have been fair. She was glad when she found it. She remembers at the time trying to figure out what it was about Hal's face that she found so attractive, so viscerally attractive. She didn't think she could attribute it to the ruggedness of his features, to the slight smile hovering over his lips, to his teeth, which were hardly perfect, not that she had ever found anything attractive in conventional perfection; she could not single out a particular feature. But a few years later, when she saw a picture of someone else, someone she didn't know, someone who was in the news, and she remembered the attraction she felt for one or two men she had met, and especially for Hal, it occurred to her that there was an air of androgyny around all of them, all the men she found attractive had something androgynous about them, and that air of androgyny she found particularly strong with Hal, yes, he had an air of androgyny about him despite his rugged facial features. Perhaps it was his slight physique that was part of the same appeal. How absurd that was, how absurd she thought that she was in her eighties when she finally realised, when she finally became aware of what it is that she finds physically attractive in a man. She remembers – why does she remember that now? – she remembers Patricia telling her of being attracted to a man who told her that he only had a couple of weeks to live. Patricia was accompanying a neighbour, a neighbour recovering from cancer to a yoga session at Maggie's, a social centre for people with cancer, and while the neighbour was attending the session, Patricia sat at a large wooden table in the garden. Opposite her there was a man in his late sixties, very thin and with what Patricia described as an extraordinary, profound face. He was leafing through a large coffee table-book on architecture. They started talking and he told her that he had been undergoing treatment for leukaemia for more than ten years, mostly in Germany, following an experimental trial, but that he had come to the end of the road. There was nothing they could do for him. He was sipping his herbal tea and had a bottle of oxygen next to him in a trolley. He had been an architect and later a jazz musician. Patricia said she was drawn to him and wished she'd had the presence of mind to tell him that. 'I might have made his last days better by loving him,' she said. Perhaps. But then, she thought, but didn't say that to Patricia, it might have been harder for him had Patricia told him about her feelings. It might have been harder knowing that he was dying when there was a woman loving him. Was it a protective, maternal instinct that generated her feelings? Patricia said her attraction for him had nothing to do with feeling sorry. But how could she know? And then there was also the fact that he used to be an architect. Patricia was an architect manqué and tended to be attracted to the real thing. But why is she thinking of that now? Is it possible to rationalise sexual attraction? There was also Patricia's grandfather. Yes, she remembers Patricia telling her how she used to be attracted, sexually attracted, to her dead grandfather, a man who had died when Patricia was fourteen, but she developed the feelings much later, when she was well into middle-age. She would look at photographs of her grandfather and fantasize about meeting a man who looked like that, a man who had all the qualities she remembered of her grandfather.

Yes, she did find Bill attractive. Patricia couldn't understand that, and she didn't know how to explain it to her. But perhaps she took it for granted that she found him attractive. She was married to him, she had to find him attractive. That's what she thought. Or perhaps she didn't think about it. Bill cared for her, and she could see that he loved her and that made him attractive. That was enough; she loved Bill because she thought he was caring. But later Bill was less caring. Or was he? He was grumpy. He was difficult. He would shout at her. He would tell her she was ignorant. Once he told her that she was scientifically illiterate. That was not attractive. But she still loved him, perhaps because she was used to thinking that she loved him. Martin said that Bill was more lost than she was, that Bill needed her more than she needed him. That was not true. At least, that's what she thought at the time. She remembers telling herself that Martin couldn't have known what went on in her marriage and, besides, Martin was angry at the time, upset with her for not allowing him to get closer to her, and she knew she couldn't take his words at face value. Yes, Bill needed her, but not as much as she needed him. Bill was a grown up, mature man, she was a child, a twenty-two-year-old orphan. Of course, she needed him more than he needed her, she used to think.

Could she still make love with someone? Could she still have sex if there was anyone to have it with? When she thinks of Hal, she has to touch herself and it feels good. It feels lovely. Her body looks different, but the need to be loved, touched, wanted, that need doesn't disappear with age. With Hal, sex was more than having orgasms. With Hal, sex was knowledge, as they say in the Bible. Sex as knowledge of oneself. Sex as knowledge of the other. She would give the rest of her life, well, one might say there was not much to give away at ninety-two, but nevertheless, she would be happy to die today if she could, in exchange, see Hal, once again. That silly thought comes to her every day now. Every day she wishes for those bargaining Greek gods. That's what she needs, a modern-day

Persephone who would take her to the world of dead souls and, instead of the warning Orpheus doesn't heed when he is collecting Eurydice, her warning would be that it was to be the last day of her life, that she had forfeited the rest, and she would agree straight away, without a moment's thought. She would lie down next to him, hold his hand, caress his face and stare into his eyes. She would not speak. She would look at him and that would be enough. If there were gods, she would pray for that.

Her lovers are dead. What about those who might have been? She wonders if Luke, Luke Bonifacci, or no, it was Lucca, he used the unusual spelling but said the teachers always forgot and called him Luke, could he still be alive? He was her age. But would he remember? Would he be able to conjure that sensation, that wonderful closeness, that wonderful attraction that she felt and she was sure he felt, that intimacy that never went beyond a single brush of the hand, a single touch on that day when she had a bad headache and was anxious and he could see that something was worrying her and she cannot remember now what it was, whether it was another month passing and her time running out, the time for her to be a mother. She didn't tell him anything but he could see that something was worrying her, that she was emotional. That touch. Sexual. Perhaps that's the only time she betrayed Bill. She betrayed him with another man without any physical contact with that man, except for a kindly touch, a touch of compassion, of care, and sympathy. And love. She remembers thinking that it was more intimate than sex with Bill. That thought was a betrayal. But Bill had gone first to the betrayal lounge. The women he paid. The dark side of Bill. Poor women in grotty hotels. Not Leopold Bloom and Circe. The dark side of Bill.

When Nick died, Marcel Gayet wrote an obituary in *the Guardian*. She was surprised when he telephoned her. He said Nick had a notebook with addresses of his friends and contacts and her name was there, together with the year when it was entered. He wondered if she could tell him anything about Nick he didn't know. He said he had tried to contact a few others, but they were either dead or had moved and were unreachable. She didn't tell him about the name for *Le Macaron Rose*, she didn't tell him about Nick's stay in Nepal because she assumed that Marcel would have known about it. Anyway, Marcel thought that she had met Nick in Oxford but, although they might have overlapped by a year or two, she didn't know him until she attended the pâtisserie course. But she didn't mention the course. She remembered running into Nick in the cook shop in Richmond, years after the course, and years after she had, as Nick said, rejected him, and after he had been unpleasant to her and made it clear that if they couldn't be lovers, they couldn't be friends either. How silly that was. How unkind. And she remembers being hurt by his words but realising that he wasn't a good person, or at least he wasn't a good person in the way he treated the women he was attracted to and she was glad that nothing had ever happened between them. But by the time when she ran into him in Richmond, they would have both licked their wounds and although she was neither pleased nor displeased to see him, in the end it was a calm, pleasant meeting. She remembers that Millie was ill at the time, not yet suffering from dementia, and Max had telephoned her to say that Millie wanted to learn to bake, wanted to learn to bake in her late sixties. Millie who had never toasted a slice of bread, Millie wanted to learn to bake and so she had gone to the cook shop to buy a few things to wish her well and to encourage her to pursue her new passion. And she remembers how she always found the cook shop, that particular cook shop, irresistible and how during her marriage she would have gone there looking for one thing and then, in addition to whatever she needed, she would have bought several other articles too and now she wonders whether that cook shop is still open since she has not been there for many years. Perhaps, for old time's sake she might ask Zach to drive her there at the weekend and they could look around and while she no longer needs anything, oh how she can never say the word need without remembering Lear's 'reason not the need', but really that cook shop had such wonderful items. You could say that many of them were not needed, that is, if one reduced the need to eat to a biological need to survive, and we just stuffed our grub into our mouths with our hands. She will ask Zach to drive her there on Saturday and she is sure there will be something lovely she can buy for Zach and Gabriel especially now that they have moved and have a big kitchen. A big kitchen makes a warm home. She has always liked large dining tables, so comforting to have space for serving food, for offering food, for sharing food. It took her years to persuade Bill that they needed a larger dining table and they had to change it several times as she could only persuade him to increase the size by a little each time. Eventually they did end up with a table that could accommodate ten people in comfort and then Bill agreed that it was a good idea and that they should have had a table like that from the start. He was not keen on having people around for dinner at first but then when he realised that it all went so well each time and that his friends enjoyed the evening and that everyone turned to him as the centre of attention, he stopped complaining and each time she suggested that they could have people around, he agreed. But even when the two of them were alone for dinner, she loved having a big table. A big dining table is the equivalent of a mother with large breasts, a mother with a soft belly and hugging arms. But she is glad her belly was not soft for most of her life; it is now, everything is soft now, maybe even her brain. When she says that to Zach, he laughs, and he says that it is the same with him. 'I keep forgetting things. I go upstairs and I have no idea what I was supposed to pick up.' But Nick at that cook shop, yes, that was the occasion when she bought a bowl for herself, a bowl that she convinced herself she needed and a bowl that made her enthusiastic about holding dinner parties of her own, dinner parties where she would be the only host. But she never did, no, she never did until Zach joined the family. While she was paying, the man at the till looked towards the door and he said, 'Mr Swinton, delighted to see you. I will be with you in a moment,' and she looked up and indeed, Nick was there, and he greeted her, as they used to, with a kiss on each cheek, a French, air-brush kiss, and the man at the till was surprised that they knew each other. And then Nick said he would be pleased to catch up with her and they could go to a café around the corner but she wasn't keen and she worried that his old hostile side might be resurrected. She reminded herself that he wasn't a good person, that he was a person who had refused to be her friend because she didn't want to be his lover and what was the point of talking to him again, she remembers thinking. But Nick used his charm to persuade her and she felt it would be rude to refuse and she really didn't want to make up an excuse; she found making up excuses demeaning as it made her feel small and that, in turn, would shake her confidence as it would make her think why should she be making an excuse, instead of openly saying she didn't wish to do something, like a strong, confident person. But then she also thought that after all those years Nick would have got over what happened, or rather what didn't happen, and there was no harm in having a quick coffee and a civilised chat. She remembers that when they sat down he asked her what she had bought and when she showed him the bowl, adding that she simply hadn't been able to resist it, which wasn't quite true, she could resist anything if she put her mind to it; she had a strong will and it gave her pride and confidence when she chose to resist something but, in the context of that conversation, it was only a saying, one of those things we say. She added that she was hoping to start having dinner parties, as she used to when her husband was alive. She remembers him saying that there was nothing wrong with treating herself to a present and he then sang the praises of the cook shop. And she told him she was surprised to see him there because she would have thought he would have gone to a trade warehouse to buy articles for his café and the kitchen and he said she was right but occasionally, such as that afternoon, he had some time off and he wanted to have a look at what the shop had to offer. 'As for dinner parties,' he added, 'as the Master says,' and then he quoted him: 'to invite people to dine with us is to make ourselves responsible for their well-being for as long as they are under our roofs.' And he said he loved that sentence and it was such a civilised thought to establish a link between the food and the well-being of one's guests. And she remembers thinking that she agreed with him and said so. He said it was one of many of the Master's thoughts that were the founding principles of *Le Macaron Rose*. She remembers asking him who the Master was and Nick was surprised that he had not told her about him before or had not mentioned him at the course. He said it was a long story but a very important story in his life; however, he was worried about boring her. She could see that he wanted to tell her and so she said that she would like to hear about the Master and she remembers that she was genuinely intrigued to find out who this Master might be. And then, she remembers, Nick told her how he applied to go to Oxford to study French. Nick paused, and she followed his eyes and she saw that outside on the pavement two, middle-aged people, very middle aged, if not old, perhaps the same age as Nick and her, had stopped and put their shopping down and had started kissing. She remembers how the two of them were looking at the couple outside and she wondered what Nick might be thinking. And then he turned towards her and said that in his teens he used to write poetry and he used to read a great deal of poetry and how he loved French poetry and that's why he wanted to study French. He had gone to Oxford because he loved Baudelaire and had read Proust but, he said, he had a feeling that the tutors at his interview didn't believe him because, as he heard from one of them later, those were the two writers that most candidates cited when they were asked why they had chosen to do the subject. But they let him in, he said. And the three years in Oxford had turned an aspiring poet into an aspiring pâtisserie chef. He said that while he was there, he learned about the sensual pleasure of desserts. He learned that sensuality, the finest sensuality, is intellectual. He learned it from his inimitable tutor, Madeleine Chambois. He said that with her, food, and especially desserts, were at the centre of profound thinking, intellectual discourse, as she used to say. That became his guiding principle. As an undergraduate, he dreamed of opening a café with exquisite cakes and welcoming her. He imagined her as a regular visitor; he would have made sure that she had her own table. He would have loved to have been able to honour her. Unfortunately, she died before he could open a café. Later, whenever he made *babas au rhum*, he wondered what she would have thought of them. He said he would never forget her tutorials and the moment when Professor Chambois announced the end of their consultation by saying that it was time for coffee and her favourite cake. Young and naïve, he was amazed to hear that the cleverest person he had ever known could harbour a weakness for confectionery. She didn't seem to be well-known in the non-academic world but one of the obituaries claimed that, 'Professor Chambois' books on the great French epicure and gastronome, have silently and almost imperceptibly percolated into English attitudes towards food, and have led to a small revolution in the way we eat and live.' Of course, he said, the TV chefs cashed in and in popular memory they are the ones who take the credit for the change in attitude. Nick said that his tutor had encouraged him to write his dissertation on *The Physiology of Taste*, the hugely influential text by Jean-Anthelme Brillat-Savarin, the Master, and he was immediately smitten by the Frenchman's combination of passion and reason. She remembers asking whether he meant Savarin, as in the baking mould. And Nick said that alas that's all that most people know about him. But he was a very learned man, his Master, a lawyer, a judge at the highest court in the land and a musician. She remembers being pleased when she heard that. Nick said that Brillat-Savarin played the violin in a theatre orchestra in New York, where he spent a couple of years in exile after the French revolution. She wondered whether the Master was a reactionary who didn't approve of the values of the Revolution, but she didn't say it. Nobody's perfect.

She remembers telling Marcel all this and he made notes as she talked. Brillat-Savarin and Professor Chambois came to feature prominently in Nick's obituary. There was even a reference to Professor's Chambois' obituary, published thirty years earlier.

There will be no obituary for her. Not even in the 'Other Lives' section. Unless Zach, or Gabriel, were to write one. After all, she is the mother-in-law to a novelist. Of course, there was an obituary for Bill. But no one spoke to her about it. A colleague of Bill's wrote the piece, focusing on his professional achievements. She was mentioned at the end as his second wife, who survived him. The only reference to the first was to say that she had predeceased him. Nothing about how and why. Bill's life was reduced to his work. It will be the same with Martin. But with her, there are no professional achievements. Zach is her only achievement. But how could Zach write about that without mentioning the Jocasta part of the story? She helped me come out. Or if Gabriel were to write it, he could say, she helped my partner come out and she helped me meet him and she helped us towards thirty years of happiness. It's a major achievement to have given someone thirty years of happiness. That's more than most people can boast. An achievement but not one that anyone could write about. Or perhaps her obituary should say she had the potential to become someone, a professional musician of some standing but she accepted her failure and she was content. Shouldn't there be obituaries about people who accepted failure? Isn't that more difficult than riding on success? A Nobel Prize for graceful failure and the acceptance of one's lot, the ultimate acceptance without regret. A Booker, a Goncourt for coming to terms with one's failure. Many entries and most well-deserving of the prize.

Why not? She remembers a friend, a writer, a poet, a wonderful poet, introducing her to a poem by Yeats, yes, 'To a friend whose work has come to nothing'. A handsome man he was. Anthony. Yes, that was his name. Could he still be around? Unlikely. Older than Martin. Very unlikely. And she remembers the lines 'Because of all things known / that is most difficult.' Most difficult, one's work coming to nothing. Yes. But . . . but, yes, she had been happy throughout her life. She had a long life, she loved and she was loved. That could be mentioned in the obituary. And she had some great sex. Gosh, everyone would be envious but no one ever writes such things in an obituary. A pity. There is something warped about our hierarchy of achievements. Oh yes, she acquired a son, and what a marvellous son, when she was sixty-three. Not many women can boast that.

❧

There was a time, soon after Zach and Gabriel got together and she could see they were happy, there was a time when she began to long for a grandchild and sometimes she would feel embarrassed as she could see herself as others might see her, an old dear talking to young mothers and peeping into their prams or when walking in the park, sometimes with Martin and Poirot, looking at the children on swings and toboggans and she wondered whether she would have preferred a little girl or a little boy, even thinking of names and wondering whether Zach and Gabriel might like the name Alba, or Phoebe, or for a boy, Gustave, or Otto, or Milo; she had always liked such names and had hoped to call her son Gustave. Like Flaubert, like Fauré, like Matoš, a Croatian poet she came to know about from a woman who was a friend many years ago, Gustave like Moreau or Doré. It was presumptuous to think like that. It would have been up to Zach and Gabriel, she knew that, she wouldn't have interfered. And she didn't. She never mentioned the idea of a child to them. She didn't want to put pressure on them. It was their life and they were happy. She couldn't have asked for more. Their happiness made her happy.

Patricia's Alba, as well as all of Patricia's grandchildren, including the younger daughter's little boy, no more than a couple of weeks' old at the time, were at the unveiling of the bench. It would have been six months, or perhaps even a year after her death. The baby must be in his late twenties now, Alba, almost forty. She wonders if Patricia's daughters are still alive. Why not, in their sixties? But their mother died at sixty-eight. Bad luck, bad luck it was. At the unveiling, she remembers thinking there was death, Patricia's death, and there was birth, the new baby: she cannot remember if he had a name then. Birth and death. The newborn coming to bow to the dead. A reversal of the Magi story, a secular reversal, that's what she thought then.

When Zach arrives, if they are not in a hurry, she will ask him to read her a poem. He reads beautifully. She will ask him to read to her 'The Love Song of J Alfred Prufrock'. They both love that poem, she and Zach. She remembers the first time she read it to him, he hadn't known it, and how they both had tears in their eyes. She was the age of Prufrock, or perhaps even older, but now it's Zach who is that age. Overnight, Zach is older than Prufrock. As for her, no one writes poems about people her age. No one writes novels about women her age. People of her age are not written about, they are written off. She remembers when she was a few years younger than Zach is now, more than thirty years ago, she read a letter in the paper, a letter by a woman exactly her age now, a letter from a woman asking how to cope with her heartache. A man she had met twenty years earlier, a man slightly younger than her and who became her lover, had recently told her that he had found someone younger and she was devastated. She used to think that when one got to old age, the woman wrote, seriously old age, one would not care. But the woman did. Of course, she did. She felt like a heart-broken teenager. What was she to do? She remembers being moved by the letter. The need for love never recedes, she knew that even then. It's just that we cope better when we don't have love in old age, or some people cope better. But even if we don't learn to cope, most older people keep to themselves their feeling of loneliness, and especially the longing for sexual love, simply because they are not expected to have such desires. The world considers it improper. That is why it is moving when someone ninety plus dares acknowledge her heartache. Poor woman, she thought then. But also, a brave woman. And now that she is ninety plus, does she feel the lack of love? Zach and Gabriel love her but they are children. Could there be anyone to love and desire her? Desire her sexually? Desire her like she and Hal desired each other. It would make her happy if she knew there was someone. There was someone. Dear Antony, the singer, the androgynous singer she loved: 'I hope there is someone. I hope there is someone when I die,' he sang. Did Martin ever desire her? Or was it simply opportunism? She was a friend, the wife of a dead friend, and she was a neighbour. They got on. It was convenient. It was practical. After all, they were eating most suppers together, spending most evenings together. Walking Martin's dog several times a week. Now, Poirot had a gentle, quiet death. And at home. She remembers Martin coming over in the middle of the day. She had just finished a lesson and the student was on the way out. Poirot had a long life, unexpectedly long for an Irish setter, sixteen years, and the vet had warned them the year earlier that the dog was old and weak and could die any time. She went over. Poirot was lying quietly in his basket, his breathing loud and laboured. Martin put on some Mozart and they stroked the dog. Soon, he closed his eyes and he died peacefully. Not a twitch. Patricia said she wanted to go like that. She remembers asking her what she meant. Lying in a dog's basket and being stroked by Martin while listening to Mozart? Patricia pulled a face. She didn't like jokes about dying. How people wish they could choose the way to die. Patricia wanting to die like Poirot, Millie wanting to die like Patricia. Absurd to say that. Neither had their wish. Patricia died alone. At least, it wouldn't have lasted long, maybe an hour, if that, but certainly not days, weeks, or years, like Millie's. But Patricia had no Mozart and no one to stroke her. Nor was she lying in her bed, like Poirot. No, she fell on the hard, wooden floor in her hall. What will hers be like? If it's quick, it's likely Zach would find her. She has a list of music for the funeral. Apart from the classics, one of Bach's cellos suites and one of Beethoven's cello sonatas – she keeps changing her mind about which ones – there is Paul Robeson, there has to be Paul Robeson, and there is Leonard Cohen, Roy Orbison. She wondered whether to play 'I'm Your Man' at Bill's funeral but wasn't sure it was his taste. Bill had no views on music, so how could she know what he liked? She didn't dare. 'Hope there is someone who will take care of me when I die.' Yes, Zach introduced her to Antony and the Johnsons and that's on the list. Goes by the name of Anohni now. And she. He or she, Anohni is most beautiful. How wonderful to have gender fluidity acceptable. Perhaps class is the last barrier. Zach will take care of her when she dies. She doesn't have to hope. She knows Zach will take care of her. Zach knows all her wishes. 'Have a good party,' she told him. And she knows he will. Perhaps, Gabriel will read something, or possibly even write something for her. Strictly secular, she told them. They were pleased with that. She is not bothered if she is cremated or not. If not, she would like one of those ecological coffins, cheap and biodegradable, and a resting place in a forest. Resting place. How ridiculous that euphemism is. What would she be resting from? Life? And when she had enough of rest, what would she do? Get up and go? She has just thought of something else. She ought to tell Gabriel. She trusts him to choose what he wishes to read, but could he also read Eliot's 'Magi' at her funeral? Or maybe Zach could. They have read enough Eliot together. Such a secular poem, she has always thought, despite Eliot's faith. The old king asking about the purpose of the journey. Isn't that the voice of someone who has lost his faith? An appropriate poem to read at her funeral. And Pound please. Perhaps 'Greek', or 'Alba'. But who would be there? Zach and Gabriel. Their friends. Most, or perhaps all, of hers have gone. Except Martin. Martin remains. She mustn't say gone. They died. To say they have gone means they could come back or that they have gone somewhere. One friend died abroad. His wife had him cremated there and then brought him back in an urn. She scattered the ashes in his favourite pub in Soho and held a wake in the same place. She recalls asking what had happened to the ashes. Someone said, 'You are standing on them.' A lovely party with speeches from his many friends and his several wives. That was a good way to remember him. But he was so young. Sixty-two. She needs to calculate how old he would have been had he lived. Yes, a hundred and one. Still younger than Martin. She had a feeling he wanted to die. All that drinking. A pity, he was a genuine person, lovely in every way, so kind, with a great gift for friendship. Why do good ones die early and bad ones stay longer? But was she bad? No rhyme or reason to how long one gets. And then the friend she met at the choir. Lymphoma. He refused treatment, saying it would have been horrific. He was low, depressed, lonely. She wished she had made an effort and been a better friend. She wished she had persuaded him to have treatment. Perhaps she should have done more things with him, taken him out, helped him realise that life could be good and that it was worth making an effort. She should have supported him better. It might have worked. He is buried in a cemetery close to his house. Late fifties he was. Much, much too young; even then she thought that. He was a year older than her. His wife only told his friends the bad news after the funeral. It was not fair, not kind. Lonely in life, lonely in death, poor David. She thought it was sad but what did it matter to him? And then Hal. Lung cancer. By the time it was diagnosed, it was too late. But he didn't tell her. She wished he had. But what would she have said? What comfort could she have offered? Tell him that she loved him and that he was the best lover she had ever known. He knew all that. Yes, but if she could have told him, it might have been some comfort. Or it might have upset him as he might have thought more about what he was losing. They were made for each other. Not to live together but made for each other to make love. When she thinks of him, she sees them locked in an amorous embrace, at the moment just before orgasm. How many times did she wish for time to stop when they were together? '*Lente lente currite noctis equi.*' Ovid has the best line about love. And then the fantasy she cannot forget: a double heart attack at the moment of orgasm and they are not found until rigor mortis has set in. Her recurring fantasy of that specially constructed coffin. But what a silly thought. Stay together forever. There is no forever. But it is also an anarchist thought, and she knows now that in her heart of hearts she is an anarchist, someone who likes to subvert social conventions, and how interesting that it took her a lifetime, and an unusually long life, to recognise – or it is to develop? – that side of herself. It took her a lifetime to shed her shyness and be open and say what she feels. Sometimes she wonders whether it would have happened had she not met Zach. And how lovely it is, that exchange between them. She helped him to be himself and then he helped her shed all the falseness that she had accumulated over the years, the years of her childhood and the years of her marriage. They gave birth to each other.

Sometimes she wonders if Bill had ever opened up to anyone. Was it in Bill's character to be remote, or did he develop that detachment, the persona he projected to the world, after the tragedy of his first marriage? Had Bill ever shared his innermost feelings with Martin? Unlikely. Which means that he had not opened up to anyone. He had certainly not spoken to her in a way that would allow him to show his fragile side. There was something in his manner that made it clear to her that he wished to keep certain parts of his life to himself. Or could it be that he wasn't aware of his vulnerability in the sense that he refused to acknowledge it to himself? What was he afraid of? She and Patricia opened up to each other. They trusted each other, trusted each other to reveal their vulnerabilities. Perhaps Bill never trusted anyone. Not his best friend, not his wife. He kept his guard. What does it mean when a man says he has a good friend? A friend you can rely upon in difficulty of any kind, and a friend in whom you confide your innermost thoughts. That's what she had with Patricia, but she doesn't think Bill and Martin had such a relationship. They were both too bloody private, closed in. She didn't like that side of Bill and she recognised the same in Martin. Patricia used to say that, like most men, the two were autistic and she felt Martin was Bill's friend for all those years because he was biding his time. Biding his time? 'Yes,' she said, 'he hoped that with Bill ten years older than him, he would outlive him. He was after you all the time but couldn't do anything while Bill was alive.' She laughed. How absurd Patricia could be! Yes, Martin had some hopes once she was widowed, but she put him right there. He wasn't happy and he sulked, but it was nothing like the nastiness of Nick, cutting her off, not answering her messages, no, but to imagine Martin would have been after her for all those years, no, Patricia had to be wrong. True, he bought a house next door to them months after they were married but they encouraged him. Martin was looking to move out of the house he had shared with his mother, and a house next to theirs came on the market. They were an elderly couple, downsizing, and she told Bill and then it was Bill's idea to tell Martin. But it didn't surprise her that Patricia had such thoughts. She could never tell why Patricia didn't like Martin. Nor could Patricia. 'I disliked him on first sight,' she used to say. She should have given him a chance. Patricia used to say that Martin and Bill were essentially two lonely people who were friends out of necessity. They needed the sense that they had a friend. They met when they were both stood up for a game of squash but later there was no necessity to continue and to continue for more than thirty years, so perhaps there was something in their relationship.

She was sad when they fell out and how wrong both of them with their assumptions about her, about life, about fiction. Writers always borrow from the lives of those around them. A story in a novel is fiction. Bill never understood about fiction. For him, it was all real, all true. But she didn't argue with him about that and now that she wonders why she didn't tell him that he was being silly, it occurs to her that in those days she behaved as if Bill knew everything. It was her fault to let him think that he knew everything. But she was happy. Bugger that. Stop saying that, Claire. You are happy now. The rest is in the past.

She has the birthday candles ready for Martin's cake: ten big ones and two small ones, in different colours. Red, green, blue and yellow. She baked the cake with the same care as she took every year, every year for the past seventy years. While Bill was alive, Martin used to invite them out for dinner on his birthday but the cake was always baked by her; they had it at home. Three almond sponges with almond cream and chocolate ganache. Chocolate glazing. It's Martin's favourite cake. Zach will bring the macarons. Three colours but Martin always chooses the green ones. Pistachio. She remembers Nick telling her about sourcing them from a grower in Sicily. He used to travel there every autumn and select a batch. Marcel has continued with the same supplier but now he buys them from the sons of the supplier. Yes, Marcel said, they have a Europe-wide distribution. Globalisation. Capitalism coming to small village producers. Last year, Martin's publisher and his agent arrived bearing a gift of champagne and a selection of their books on audio. Martin's eyes are too poor for him to read and so it's either audio or, if that is not available, he pays a young student to read to him. The chap comes twice a week and they read mostly detective fiction. Martin no longer writes but last year he told his agent, yes, at the party, he told his agent that he had an idea for a children's book. The agent encouraged him to get on with it. He didn't sound surprised. She was amazed. Martin has never been in contact with any children. If anything, he finds children annoying. But maybe that would not stop him from writing a good story for children. Why should it? It's like saying the writer has to be the same age, sex, gender and race, and whatever else, as their protagonist. Limiting essentialism, that's what it is, she has always thought, but these days many people wouldn't agree. Martin has a wonderful imagination. Those sixty novels, sixty and a bit, didn't come out of nowhere. Yes, there was a formula to them, the rules of the genre, but the stories came from his head. And from people's lives but you need imagination to know what to use and how to transform it. That's probably even harder than making it up from scratch.

Does Martin still want her to help him with the list of music for his funeral? Years ago, he said he would draft it and then he would like her to go over it, make suggestions, finalise it. He mentioned it several times over the years. And whenever she said they should do it, he would laugh and say there was time and she wondered whether he was superstitious, whether he thought he might keep death waiting by postponing his funeral preparations. She will not ask, not today of all days. Bill didn't have a list but that didn't stop him dying. Bill would never have thought of making one. He knew, if it ever crossed his mind, that she would do it for him, and do it better than he could have. Music wasn't important to him. Except when she played. He used to tell her that. Sometimes in the evening, on those evenings when he didn't work in his study, he would sit on the sofa in her piano room and listen to her. He said he found it relaxing. More often than not, he fell asleep. That was hardly flattering, but she understood. He was tired. He worked hard. They were happy. For Bill, music provided a background, as in a film where music manipulates the emotions. She doesn't like that. She finds it false. Of course, there are exceptions. She prefers to hear what the character hears. If no music plays for the character, there should be none for the spectator. People assumed she would play at his funeral. One of Bill's colleagues, one of those who would have heard the story of their meeting many times, told her they had all expected to hear her play. They had no understanding of feelings. Playing is emotional. How could she had done it when she was the principal mourner? Yes, the principal mourner, that's what the funeral directors called her. She was too distressed to do anything so emotionally exigent. She was full of Bill, and she wanted to be with him in her thoughts, too occupied with him to be able to focus on playing. But she was glad there was live music. People said it was unusual. But they liked it as it created a special atmosphere, uplifting and comforting. Was there music in the lounge when Bill died? Poirot had music when he died. She cannot remember if there was music when Bill died. She was angry and couldn't have cared less if anything was playing in the lounge. But it's a good idea to have music in hospitals, when people are dying to comfort them. Music didn't comfort Bill. It put him to sleep.

And when she thinks of that evening, she has questions but no answers. He was angry and he was grumpy and he shouted at her. He called her ignorant. She was upset, of course she was. It wasn't the first time he had treated her so badly but she could never get used to his manner. She couldn't think clearly. She gave him the pills when he asked for them. She was sure he had already taken them but she didn't say it. There was no point arguing with him, let alone when he was in such a cantankerous mood. And she left him. Yes, she heard the thump. He uttered a cry but she couldn't think clearly and she ignored whatever was going on in the lounge. She needed to dissociate herself from whatever was happening. She dialled Patricia. Patricia was surprised she had called so early. Usually, they spoke later in the evening. They stayed talking for over an hour and Patricia commented that it was good to talk without interruptions, without Bill coming and asking whether they would be long. She remembers her friend saying that and she remembers talking at length and yet, all the while, she was tense. She was tense but tried to relax, tried not to think about whatever was going on or had gone on in the lounge, except the conversation. Patricia was in a good mood and she recounted at length her latest date and they laughed as they had not laughed for a long time. Was her laughter a nervous response? The laughter of tension?

Before that evening, she had been concerned because there had been several evenings when he had forgotten to take his pills. The packets had days of the weeks indicated on them, but he would press out any pill, not the one for that day and often his boxes were in disarray and one couldn't tell what had been taken and what hadn't. That was very much unlike Bill she used to know for many years earlier. He became impatient and grabbed whatever fell out of the foil. He wouldn't always count. You would have thought a doctor would know what he was doing, but he was too grouchy to care. Too angry. But what was he angry about? That he was ageing? That's what Patricia thought. 'He sees how young and lovely you are, still in your prime, and then he looks at himself and he resents you.' At the time, she thought Patricia was wrong. She loved him, or so she thought, and her view was that, if anything, Bill should have rejoiced that she loved him, old or not. In any case, she didn't think he was old. Ill-tempered, yes. But he could choose not to be. She never commented on his grumpiness and tried not to think about it, but it was hard to cope with constant rudeness and that evening she might have had enough. At first, she thought he was tense because of the flight next morning, but then she lost patience and, unusually for her, she stopped making excuses on his behalf.

But she doesn't remember clearly what happened with the pills. After all, she was rushing and he was shouting and she had no idea what he took. Perhaps he swallowed several days' worth of medication. A good handful it was. And he had already taken what she thought was twice his required evening dose. She watched him as he swallowed them all in one go. She remembers that when he finished, he faced her squarely, looked into her eyes, which was the first time he had looked at her that evening, and after a few moments' pause, he said he was ready. And it was that gesture of staring into her eyes, and the pause, the theatrical pause, the pause for effect that loaded the situation and abolished the possibility of her thinking that he was ready for bed or for the trip or something similarly mundane. No, it was clear he was ready for something bigger. Something serious. And to make sure that she understood, he took on a role, the role of accusing her of something, no matter what, the role of being hostile to her. That's why he stared at her. And yet she wondered what he meant. Ready for what? But she didn't dare ask. Bill repeated that he was ready. Another pause. And then he said he knew she had heard him the first time. He meant what he said. He was ready. He said he was ready and that meant he was ready. She refused to engage with his game. She thought it was nothing but a silly game. One of those games that Bill increasingly resorted to in the last years of their life together. One of those games that always made her anxious. The only way she could stop the tightening in her chest was to refuse to play. She left the room to deal with the dishwasher. And sometime between starting the dishwasher and going to her piano room, she heard a cry and then a thump. Bill fell on the floor. She saw him lying on the floor when she walked past the open door of the lounge.

Next morning, after the police had gone, she sat alone for a couple of hours before Martin arrived in a taxi – he was away for a day attending the funeral of a publisher – and knocked on the door. And she remembers hearing Bill's voice during those solitary hours calling her 'my dear, little Claire' and it distressed her. But he kept calling and his voice was heart-rending. She was hurting but she could not cry. And when the police spoke to her a second time, a few days after the autopsy, and asked her whether Bill had talked about suicide, she thought it was an absurd question. They had been very happy. That is what she thought then and that is what she told them. He had completely recovered from his stroke and there was nothing she could think of that might have made him want to die. The police asked whether they had argued and she said they hadn't. You couldn't call that little disagreement an argument. And Bill saying, 'I am ready', that was a silly game of no significance; there was no point mentioning it. They wouldn't have understood Bill's usual histrionics. When she had eventually asked what he was ready for, he had not replied. So, it didn't mean anything. It wasn't worth mentioning. Who knows what they might have constructed out of that insignificant sentence?

She really couldn't have played at his funeral. She asked a professional cello player to play. After all, the cello is a more emotional instrument than the piano, an instrument to conjure tears, and she thought Bill would have liked everyone to cry, enjoying his last display of power. The cellist was a few years younger than her but he died soon after Bill's funeral. A couple of weeks later. She remembers going to his funeral. That was suicide. He had suffered from depression for many years and had left a note. Another cellist played there. Could that one be still alive?

She remembers her cellist boyfriend during the strange year she spent in Paris. Guillaume asked to accompany her on the cello when he heard her play Sati's *Gymnopédie*, the music she played more often than any other at that time after the death of her parents. Guillaume became a kind of boyfriend. She had lapsed by then, but he was a Catholic and very observant. More observant than her parents even. They held hands but never kissed properly and certainly nothing more intimate. So much for French lovers. She was annoyed with him. She wanted him to desire her. And maybe he did but his faith was stronger, the prohibitions of his faith. How ridiculous that sounds, what is the point of prohibitions that make people unhappy? She left him. And then he died of grief. Seventy odd years ago. A lifetime of being dead. She felt he died of grief and blamed herself. She remembers that a huge American student, Nancy, told her that Guillaume had a congenital heart condition. She said it was a miracle he had lived into his mid-twenties. Quite likely. But at the time she was sure she had killed him. Her parents and then the young Frenchman. She saw herself as a serial killer. Following Guillaume's death, she had made that absolutely ridiculous vow of chastity. How stupid youth can be. So it was no wonder she tried to be a good little girl with Bill. She never mentioned Guillaume to Bill. He would have laughed at her for thinking herself responsible. Or he might have said he wished she had a more rational mind. Or he might even have been jealous of the poor dead Frenchman, like Gabriel in Joyce's story 'The Dead'.

The year in Paris, a year of frustrated desire. She remembers the large house where she rented a room, sharing facilities with other young people. She remembers at night hearing lovers in the adjoining rooms. She was always alone and had developed her own pleasure game. She would eat two green macaroons, slowly, savouring every crumb, letting the almond pastry melt in her mouth, and then she would pull the blanket over her head and touch herself, touch herself until she too, like her neighbours, had an orgasm. Pistachio macarons were the foreplay. She foreswore them when she heard of Guillaume's death. She kept her promise for forty years, until the box arrived from Nick. Even then, she hesitated for a few days before she took one out, goaded by Patricia, making fun of her self-prohibition. How Patricia loved the macarons. She said she would gladly go out with Nick if he baked like that. Alas, Nick showed no interest in her.

That year of frustrated desire. Young and in Paris and yet. She can only call herself a slow learner. It took her, what was it, forty odd years before she learned what she wanted. Mr Gintz and his *nosce te ipsum*. Sixty odd years to relax, to learn to relax and find out who she was. Or who she could be.

❧

She broke that silly vow of chastity with Bill, a couple of months before they were married. She was a virgin, but Bill didn't realise. She never bled. She never bled, not even before when she had boyfriends who penetrated her with their fingers. Perhaps she wasn't a virgin when she was born. 'What a terrible thing for a Catholic girl,' Patricia said and laughed. She bled, Patricia said, it was a real massacre how much she bled. A blood bath. And how it hurt. 'You were lucky.' 'Why?' 'Lucky because it didn't hurt and lucky, really lucky, because no man could claim to have conquered you.' She thought it was funny, but Patricia said it wasn't a joke. It was important. If she could turn the clock back, Patricia used to say, she would have taken her own virginity. She remembers a story Patricia once gave her to read, a story about a visitor being taken through a gallery exhibiting the sheets used by noble families on the wedding night. The sheets are framed and each carries a red stain, signifying the consummation of marriage. But then the visitor comes to a white, immaculate sheet. What does that sheet stand for? Was the woman not a virgin or was the marriage not consummated and, whatever the answer, it raises the further question as to why. Patricia loved it. 'A blank sheet on which no man has written with his pen.'

After their first time, Bill assumed she wasn't a virgin and when she explained, he said it was extremely rare for a woman not to bleed. Had she lived in different times or in a different culture, it would have been a problem, he said. He didn't say so, but she could see that he also thought she was lucky, but in a different way, lucky because she was with a man for whom it wasn't important. She doesn't recall she ever had an orgasm with Bill. At the beginning, to start with, she was too inhibited and inexperienced, and she wanted to please him so she faked it. She wished she hadn't. She wished she had had the courage and knowledge to speak to him. To explain what was going on. But she felt too ashamed and, besides, she didn't know what would give her pleasure. She never had an orgasm with a man. Not until Jon. But maybe she is being unfair, maybe she is misremembering. There were occasions when she managed to get excited; she remembers once seeing two dogs at it and the sight of them turned her on and next time when she and Bill were making love, she remembered the dogs. Maybe she did come then and a few other times, but it wasn't powerful. Her orgasms were not intense. It took the man on Petersham Road for that. But the occasional lovers after him were not much. Nothing until Hal. He was a master, a professor of lovemaking. And even if he hadn't done anything, she could have come just by looking at his face. He was the only lover she had known who liked to do exactly the same things as her. That was perfect although with him it hardly mattered as she was prepared to do anything. She remembers sitting in the pew at St Martin's and listening to Vivaldi – or was it Bach? – and she had a vision of having oral sex with the man next to her. That was extraordinary. She was excited by the image of her sucking him. It was extraordinary because she had always disliked oral sex. She disliked giving it, she disliked receiving it. She was too squeamish for either. Hal had the same reservations. And yet, with him she could have done anything. With anyone else, she had to be cajoled into it. She would do it to please Bill but she always felt uncomfortable, counting the seconds, hoping he would soon have had enough. She and Hal established that preference the first time and it didn't have to be mentioned again. She could never understand that women would actually get pleasure from sucking a man's penis. Sometimes she wondered whether it had anything to do with being breastfed in infancy or sucking one's thumb. She wasn't breastfed. Her mother told her it wasn't the fashion at the time she was born. Only peasant women were supposed to breastfeed their children. Of course, it all changed later, completely so by the time she was hoping to have a child. And her parents actively discouraged her from sucking her thumb when she was a baby. Maybe she never developed that habit of sucking, maybe her feelers for sucking have remained dormant. She remembers a man she was corresponding with during her dating phase, a man she never met but who told her of his experience with another man. He claimed he wasn't gay but wanted to have that experience and so he arranged for a threesome with a female friend, and an occasional lover of the female friend, another man. He said that at some point he was asked to suck the man and that while he felt revulsion, he obliged, as he wished to be cooperative, since it was his idea. Afterwards it took him days before he was comfortable holding his own penis when peeing. He said he had asked one of his female friends what it was that women found pleasurable in giving oral sex and that she was amazed at his need to ask that question. 'Isn't it obvious,' she responded but didn't say anything specific. Well, it's never been obvious to her. She has always thought that it was one of those myths than men liked to propagate, saying that women were gagging for it, hah, that's a funny word, part of the myth that made women who didn't conform to that expectation feel insufficient, thinking that they were lacking in something, and in order to avoid being considered insufficient, most women went along and carried on sucking penises while hating it. None dared say what they really felt. A case of the emperor's new clothes, if ever there was one. Patricia used to say it was a question of what kind of man and what kind of penis. 'Some were uglier than others,' she claimed. She remembered one man whose penis was beautiful, much paler than others, average or good size but not too thick, not too long. Smooth. 'A French guy it was,' Patricia said. 'A great penis but a difficult man.' That was very much a Patricia sentence. How she misses her. At the time, she wondered whether Patricia was very observant or whether it was all in her imagination. But she couldn't argue with Patricia's view that there was a design fault with male bodies. The penis sticking out spoiled the harmony of the body. Shouldn't it have been somewhere inside to be pulled out when required? No wonder Michelangelo's David has such a tiny one. A small appendage in order not to upset the composition. There is little harmony in an average male body. She has always found it pleasurable, and exciting, to see a naked woman, but never a man. And yet, she has never desired a woman. Or perhaps, as Patricia would say, 'the right woman never came along.' She will never know.

When was the last time she used the vibrator? Not that she needs to ration herself. She uses it whenever she feels like it. A handy little gadget. Sometimes a couple of weeks pass, and she doesn't feel the need and at other times it may be several days in a row. Is it to do with her memories or her hormones? That is, if she still has any hormones. Memories of her time with Hal turn her on. That's what she thinks of when she lies down. Of course, she thinks of Hal. There were one or two men after his death, but she didn't expect anyone to replace Hal. When he died, it was all finished for her. No one stood a chance.

Zach always texts before he comes to see her. He texts even when she is expecting him. He texts when he is close to the house, a couple of minutes' away or so. He respects her privacy. He would not want to embarrass her by walking in on her when she is using the vibrator, she imagines. And when he texts, she responds, just so that he knows she is fine. At her age, who knows what could happen. And if she didn't respond, what would he do? Would he still use the key, or would he call 999 before going in?

Perhaps Zach and Gabriel could take her to Florence for a few days in the spring. She will mention it to them today. She could travel on her own, she could still just about travel on her own, but it would be much nicer to look at Leonardo's 'Magi' at the Uffizi with the two of them. She remembers the first time she and Zach went, before Gabriel joined the family, and she was so keen to show Zach the painting, one of her favourites, certainly one of the most moving pictures ever, a picture that, in her mind, accompanies Eliot's 'Magi'. They walked through the whole gallery, keeping Leonardo's room to the end, as one keeps the best morsel of food to last, and then when they entered the room, she thought she knew exactly on which wall the painting was hanging. But it wasn't there. Zach had never seen it, not in real life, and she so much wanted to share it with him but the painting wasn't there. Maybe it had been moved to another wall? No, it is a large canvas and a glance around told her that couldn't have been the case. Where was it? They spoke to an assistant. The painting was being restored. But they had come specially to see it. They will have to return to Florence, the woman said. And they did, a year later. She remembers they booked into a small hotel not far from the Ponte Vecchio and it was clear that the woman at the reception assumed they were mother and son. A couple of years earlier, she would have baulked at such an assumption, an assumption based on the prejudice that an older woman wouldn't have a younger partner, but by that time she felt proud to be seen as Zach's mother. Who would have thought that after a lifetime of sadness at having missed motherhood, she would finally achieve it? Sometimes she wonders what Bill would think if he were to see her and the idea makes her smile. She is her own woman now, not his 'lost, little girl'.

The second time at the Uffizi, they went straight to Leonardo. The last time she saw the painting would have been twenty odd years earlier. The juxtaposition of the old bony heads, skulls really, of the three kings, and that of the plump, doll-like body of the baby with its smooth skin, struck her even more powerfully than before. She couldn't see what it had to do with the representation of the story from the Bible. It was a lament on old age. She once shared her view of the painting with an art historian who told her that the painting was not finished and therefore we couldn't interpret

Leonardo's intention. What a silly thing to say! Who cares about intentions? They have a painting, finished or unfinished and that painting has a meaning.

She has always felt that the narrator in Eliot's poem is someone who has lost his faith. The same sentiment was present in the painting. It couldn't have been created by an artist whose faith was unshaken. Leonardo might have lost it by that time. There is no joy, magic, or expectation on the faces of the old kings. They know that only death awaits them, no eternal kingdom. They know they will die soon and then there will be nothing. She remembers Zach saying that, in his view, only an artist with a strong personality could come to terms with the idea, let alone represent it, that there was no eternal life. No one weak would dare. Not at the time. She and Zach wondered whether the Church would have found it sacrilegious. Or could this only be seen by those who have no faith themselves? She remembers saying that she wanted to find out but somehow it slipped her mind. Perhaps that should be her next project. She will start on the Internet tomorrow and perhaps order some documents, see what's available from the British Library. She has been lucky with her eyes. She can still read. All she needs are her reading glasses and good light. She was lucky not to have needed reading glasses until she was in her mid-sixties. Everyone else she knew relied on them as soon as they passed fifty. Her genes or those green vegetables? Kale, lots of kale and cavolo nero and chard. It's good that Zach and Gabriel have developed a taste for it.

❧

It's a sunny day outside, a great day for a party. They might even be able to sit on the patio outside Martin's room. She has always felt that sunny days are not for death, they are for births. They are for starting anew. She remembers reading a description somewhere, many years ago, of Eugene Delacroix's funeral. It rained heavily and, allegedly, Manet, one of the mourners, said that it was a good day for a funeral. Was he thinking of Verlaine's 'il pleure dans mon cœur comme il pleut sur la ville'? Is that the right line? She must check. Zach would know. His French is better than hers. But perhaps Delacroix had died before the poem was written. Yes, she must check that too. Whenever she attended a funeral on a rainy day, she would remember Verlaine's line. Bill had no French. She felt sorry for him. He was missing so much. But he would have said the same about her, complaining about her wild fantasies, her lack of a scientific mind. At least Nick had perfect French and he read poetry. She remembers the day when they met at the National Gallery after he had asked her to help him with Monet's water lilies. She shared his view that reproducing Monet, or any artwork, on a cake, would mean, as he put it, she remembers his words, selling out to Disney. She wanted to make a joke and say that Monet was hardly Mickey Mouse. Was it snobbish to think that works of art should not be reproduced on everyday objects? She had an aversion to images from artworks appearing on shopping bags, umbrellas, mugs, all that stuff. So much Monet was used like that. Nick had a contract and he had no choice but to honour it, she remembers telling him. In fact, there is art that works when reproduced. Lots of Russian constructivism and suprematism works well on dishes, useful objects, yes. She had a Lissitzky mug. She bought it in Boston, at the Museum of Fine Arts. No, that was the Rothko mug. The Lissitzky she bought at the Pompidou. Yes, she still has it. But that time, she remembers Nick saying that when it came to art, he suffered from the equivalent of being tone-deaf. That was funny. But easy to sort out, she said. Unlike in music. Tone-deaf is tone-deaf. You could look at pictures without having an education in art history. You can learn how to look. Everyone should. If schools were to teach visual education, so much ugliness in daily life could be avoided. She finds the visual ugliness in the daily lives of most people depressing, from the way they dress, or even worse, the way they undress their misshapen bodies on warm days, to the way they ruin their living spaces with clutter. She remembers telling

Nick to start by registering his emotional response by comparing it to his own vision of what pleased him. He said he had no vision, no idea of what he liked. That couldn't have been true. Not a man who made those beautiful cakes, beautiful to look at, as well as to eat. He should just ask himself whether he liked a picture or not, she told him. Yes or no, that's all. And then he could try to explain his answer. As simple as that. But the problem with well-known works of art, such as Monet's, is that they are too familiar, and it is difficult to look at them afresh; there is too much baggage. As they looked at the three paintings, she suggested that he moved from judging the image and started to ask how it was constructed, how its composition worked and paid attention to the variations in colour and the brush strokes. Which of those elements contributed to what he liked or didn't like about a particular canvas? That was the question he should be asking. He seemed grateful to her and sent her more macarons to say thank you. At that time, she remembers, she wasn't sure whether Nick was a possibility on the relationship front. Patricia was around in a flash. And at that time Martin also fell in love with macarons. An intrigue around a secret macaron recipe is at the core of one of his later novels. There can't be many detective stories based around macarons. Sherlock Holmes and the Pistachio Macarons. No, that's not Martin's, just her being silly. She will tell Gabriel. He could write a spoof. Except that's not his style. But perhaps he might like to write something very different. Under a different name, if he wanted to. Create a different literary persona, subvert the maxim *le style c'est l'homme même*. Why not? Like Romain Gary with his Emil Ajar, or Cesare Pavese or that Mexican poet. Or was it the Portuguese? Yes, Pessoa. She will mention it to Gabriel. He is always happy to hear her ideas. He has even used a couple of them. And she was acknowledged for that. She loves reading him, she loves talking about his work and she loves him, and she loves Zach.

She remembers it was a sunny morning, a sunny Sunday morning like today and she was shocked how late it was when she woke up. Shocked and frightened to have broken her routine, the ritual, as she used to call it. The first morning after. Thirty years ago. She remembers she was about to get out of bed and, as she sat up, a trickle, a warm sticky trickle tickled the inside of her thighs. The male smell. It hit her then. The surprise that she had done it. The sadness that she had done it. And the joy. What joy! She felt all three together. But no, she misremembers, she wasn't shocked. She broke the routine, but it shocked her that she wasn't shocked. Was that really her, the night before, she wondered? She had had a few glasses of wine, but she wasn't drunk, she was fully aware of what she was doing. The wine had relaxed her, freed her from her inhibitions. She remembers thinking, and that shift in thinking, she could see that later, that shift was the beginning of her new life. She was no longer a widow, she was a single woman. The shift also meant, she could see that later, the beginning of finding herself, the self that was buried somewhere under the exterior of Bill's 'dear, little Claire', buried under the public image of Bill's 'lost, little girl'. But she could not ignore the sadness. Why sadness? Sadness for leaving behind her past life? No, definitely not. Bill had been dead for ten years, it was not a question of betraying him. And then there was fear. Fear of the unknown. Fear of what she might have set in motion. Perhaps it was melancholy. There certainly was joy and excitement. Yes joy, joy at the expectation of what might happen, that's what she wants to remember. She heard the telephone ringing and then there was Patricia saying how relieved she was to hear her. She had been ringing for a while and there had been no answer. Had she been in the garden? But no, her voice sounded as if she had just woken up. Was she not well? That wasn't like her to be in bed past midday, Sunday or no Sunday. She remembers considering what to say, whether to tell Patricia what happened the night before but then deciding against it. She feared being teased. She feared Patricia telling her that it was precisely what she needed. And she began to wonder whether what she thought happened had really happened, happened to her, or if she had dreamt it. But she did tell her later, a week later when she expected Jon to get in touch, and he hadn't, and she was anxiously waiting for the phone to ring. An anxious teenager of sixty-two. And then when the phone did ring, and he said he was going to be in Richmond to see his dentist, she didn't answer it as she was teaching, and she had to ring him back, but she decided not to rush into it and to make him wait, wait for a couple of days. She was aware she was engaging in a stupid, childish game. She didn't think adults should play such games and yet she did, she did because she thought he had played a game with her. But that Sunday morning, she made a cup of tea and stayed in bed, reading, luxuriating in leisure. She felt a touch of guilt, but she knew that finally she was free from rituals, from the order of her previous life. She was a single woman. She was a single woman for the first time in her life. When she met Bill, he was right to say that she was a 'lost, little girl', lost in the ways of the world. All she had were her dreams of becoming a concert pianist and perhaps a mother. But they were only dreams. She remembers Martin turning up at the usual Sunday afternoon hour for their walk in the park and she opened the door, still in her dressing gown, and him making a face and saying he hoped she was not ill. She remembers she smiled and said that she had taken the morning off to read in bed and she had done it for no particular reason. Just because she felt like it. And she remembers Martin saying that it was very much unlike her and wondering whether something had happened. And she laughed and said that she could see no reason why she had to carry on doing things in the same way as she has always done them and Martin saying that the change in her behaviour was a bit like when a woman suddenly alters her hairstyle and that means that she has a new romantic interest. She laughed loudly. A romantic interest? That was a funny phrase. And Martin wondering whether it was the wrong way of saying it because he had just used the phrase in his writing that very morning. She remembers laughing but also thinking how, despite living like a hermit in the world of his fiction, Martin had a certain worldly perspicuity. She remembers mentioning that to Patricia and Patricia had dismissed it as pure coincidence, as a revealing example of how he was really after her and felt threatened by the possibility that she might have met someone. That afternoon she told Martin she would be ready within minutes, which she was, and they went for their usual walk with Poirot. On the way out she grabbed a scarf, an expensive designer scarf Bill had brought her from his conference in Paris, the same scarf she had worn the evening before and she felt a hard patch on it as if it had been starched. Hiding her face behind the cupboard door in the hall, she brought the scarf to her nose and then she knew. That male smell again. More evidence from the night before. She wasn't ashamed at what had happened, but for a moment, she was gripped by anxiety at the thought that Bill would be annoyed; the thought crossed her mind that Bill would be annoyed that she had ruined his gift and she had to remind herself that she was free and didn't have to worry about what he thought of her. Perhaps there was something symbolic in Bill's present to her being stained with another man's sperm. Martin saw her holding the scarf and he could tell that she was hesitating what to do, so he said that it was warm outside and that she didn't need the scarf. She dropped it in the cupboard. She feared that Martin might pick it up, smell it and then, who knows? Would he have guessed the provenance of the hard patch? She remembers that she feared his questions about the night before and to prevent that, she asked him about the novel he was writing. Immediately, he launched into a detailed account of the plot. Unwittingly, she switched off and when he asked her what she thought, she remembers feeling ashamed not to be able to come up with anything better than that awfully meaningless word: interesting. But Martin was kind and generous and didn't complain. He asked her whether she could guess who the murderer was. She said the only name she could remember. Martin laughed, saying that he couldn't have done it because he was away at the time. She mentioned another name. Martin looked at her. He said the character wasn't in the novel. She must have been confusing it with one of his previous ones. And so it went on until he turned towards her and asked her whether she was all right. She didn't dare admit she had not been listening. She will listen to him this afternoon. He might even have something to read out. Apparently, he has been recording stories and the young student has been transcribing them. Gabriel was asked to help with the editing and he told her they were short pieces but he didn't wish to reveal more. It was to be a surprise. One of several surprises at the party. Martin's surprise. The others, she heard, are to be revealed by Martin's old publishers. It will be exciting. Everyone will have a surprise for Martin and he will have a surprise for everyone. It will be a good party. A joyous party. A party to remember.

There is still more than four hours before Zach and Gabriel arrive. She needs to check the cake, make sure the glazing is okay. It shouldn't have lost its shine. She must remember to pack the cake knife, only her knife would do. Anything else might not cut smoothly and she wants it to be perfect. After all, she has two certificates for successfully completing pâtisserie courses, both signed by the master pâtissier, Nick Swinton of the famous *Le Macaron Rose*. She has her reputation, not to mention his, to uphold. She dares not have such a thought, but you never know, it could be the last time someone who cares makes Martin a cake. Unless she starts teaching Zach. He would like to be able to bake, he said. But when she is no longer around, meaning when she is dead, how easily one falls into euphemisms, Zach and Gabriel would order a cake for Martin. She knows they would. This afternoon they will take photographs. They always do. She will look at the old ones before she gets up. Photographs. She remembers a writer she liked, many years ago, she remembers him asking someone whether they had come by train or by photographs. The person looked puzzled. By train or by photographs, the writer repeated his question, because, as he said, photographs are a form of transport. They transport us in time, and then they make us feel absence. 'And we all get off at the same station,' the writer said, she remembers. Martin has kept his good china, his mother's china, and that's what they will use to serve the cake and tea. Martin's mother is the only woman he ever mentioned. She didn't know her. She died around the time of her meeting Bill. Martin used to live with her and that's why once she died, he wanted to move and that's how he became their next-door neighbour. Apparently, his mother was good at baking and sometimes she wondered whether that was one of the things Martin liked about Bill's wife. Her baking. But how unusual that he kept several of his mother's dresses, very elegant, long dresses, with lace and silk, the type she imagines women used to wear to the opera. Bill said that a character based on Martin's mother appeared in several of his novels and the cover of one of them, yes, it's *This is a Red Handbag*, carries a picture of a black velvet dress. She remembers wondering whether that was a reference, no matter how oblique, to Magritte's *ceci n'est pas une pipe*, and mentioned it to Martin who hadn't thought of it before and said the cover was a clue to what happens in the story. Martin's mother always baked a cake for his birthday and made him blow out the candles. She remembers Martin telling her about his mother's cakes and birthday candles soon after she was married. She realised his birthday was only a couple of days ahead. She spoke to Bill and asked him if he thought she should bake a cake. Bill shrugged and said she wasn't Martin's mother and that he was old enough to get used to not having her around. She remembers thinking that was a bit harsh and baked a cake anyway. She and Bill went over and lit the candles. Martin was moved and that's how they established the tradition. Seventy odd cakes or so. She hasn't counted but it must be something like that. Give or take one or two. Maybe even exactly seventy. Gabriel might write a story about that. There must be pictures of all of them. Even those secret birthdays after Martin and Bill had fallen out. She would bake in secret, start as soon as Bill left in the morning and then go over to

Martin's house with the cake and candles before Bill returned. Once she had to ask Patricia if she could use her oven as Bill was at home in the morning. It was then that Patricia told her that she should be careful. 'Martin is alone, he will fall in love with you. No surer way to make a man fall in love with you than replacing his mother, let alone, baking like her,' Patricia said. And she repeated that later, after Bill's death. Martin has been biding his time, that's what Patricia thought. Seventy years of Martin's birthday cakes. Seventy years of blowing candles. Who knows what wishes he makes? What wish would he make today? To die like Patricia. Yes, he was kind to her when Patricia died. Said he was sorry. 'Terrible to die before reaching seventy,' he said. Seventy years of birthday cake pictures too. She will speak to Gabriel. Perhaps he could write one of those books with photographs, one of those that abolish the division between fiction and non-fiction. Or perhaps a graphic novel.

Zach has told her not to worry. If she dies before Martin, he and Gabriel would make sure that Martin has a party every year. That's lovely. And why is she now hearing Patricia's voice about what plans she has for her future? Plans? Her future is this afternoon's birthday party. Plans? One doesn't have plans at ninety-two. But no, she mustn't get morbid. She has more plans than she had thirty years ago.

❧

Plans. She will talk to Gabriel about a birthday book, one of those with photos, *à la* Sebald. Gabriel loves Sebald and so does she. And they will go to the cook shop soon and she will buy a present for them. Now that they have a big kitchen, they have space for all those things she wanted to buy for them. And they will go to Florence. *Firenze.* How everything sounds special in Italian. They will go to Florence, to Sienna and to Luca. She remembers Lino, the waiter who worked at a restaurant where she and Bill used to go. He was from Luca. Lino from Luca. She wonders if Bill noticed her looking at Lino. She thought him lovely. No, she wasn't attracted to him in any sexual sense, but she thought him sweet, the kind of young man she would like to hug. A motherly hug. And then one evening at the restaurant, he came to their table and told her that he was leaving and going back to Italy. He wanted to say goodbye. Leaving? Yes, he had a little daughter, Giovanna, nine months she was, and he didn't want her to grow up in gloomy London. He had sent her and his wife, he had sent her and his wife, he said, and she thought how Italian, how Italian male it was to say he had sent them, he, the man of the family had made the decision for his wife and daughter, he had sent them to Luca. Or no, maybe he said he was from Naples, yes, it was Naples, not Luca, why is she thinking of Luca, definitely Naples because she remembers telling him she had been to Naples and to Sorrento and how she found Naples scary but loved Sorrento and she told him she remembered passing by the door of Torquato Tasso's house and he asked her how come she knew of Tasso and she said that she had read parts of *Gerusalemme Liberata*. He liked that, and his eyes were dancing happily as he was looking at her and he said he didn't think Naples was scary and she felt sorry to have said that, so she told him how much she liked Capodimonte and how Caravaggio was one of her favourite painters. She remembers she could see how happy he was to hear that, this young Italian, proud of his country, a sentiment she could never share but didn't mind with this lovely, simple man and she was happy for him. Yes, simple, in the sense of uncomplicated, kind and sweet. Genuine. Genuine is important. And then she remembered a sentence she read in a novel, a novel which was in English but had a sentence in Italian and she used to think it was beautiful, both the meaning and its sound. She said it aloud for the waiter. *Solo la mente più vincere la forza di gravita.* She was pleased with her accent, her accent in Italian, which she has never studied, but always felt comfortable with because she had studied Latin, and he repeated the sentence and in his Italian mouth it sounded more beautiful than when she said it. And then he asked her whether it was from Galileo, whether the sentence was from Galileo, which she thought was funny. But sweet. Then he had to go, and she stood up and kissed him on both cheeks and he apologised that he was sweaty and she said that was fine and it was fine kissing him on both cheeks in the middle of the restaurant, with Bill sitting opposite her at the table and not saying anything. This was his 'mad, little Claire' because sometimes she was his 'mad, little Claire', just sometimes. And yes, Zach and Gabriel will take her to Italy. Would Lino still be alive? In his sixties, or seventies. Why not? And Giovanna, little nine-month-old Giovanna, the daughter of Lino would be in her forties. A mother, perhaps even a grandmother. Sometimes she has a fantasy in which all the people she has ever known, or those she has known and loved, come together in the same room after all these years and just for a day, just for a brief time, they 'catch up', and she finds out what has happened to them. Wouldn't that be lovely? All the people she remembers, dead and alive, all of them coming together.

And she has other plans after their Italian trip. One day they will return to the Prado. The three of them. She wants to see 'Las Meninas' one last time. One last time. What a silly thing to say. But yes, the Prado. Yes, that's the plan. That's her plan at ninety-two. And as they have done before, they will send postcards to Martin, each of them will send a postcard to Martin each day while they are away and when they return Martin will have them all on display, thirty or forty postcards even and they will tell him about their journey. That's what they always do.

'What are your plans?' Or sometimes, 'just tell me, how do you see your future?', were the questions Patricia asked within months of Bill's death. And she tried to make a joke and tell her that she would wash her hair, then make something for dinner and then read a book and Patricia said that she was asking a serious question and that it was about time she made some plans. And she said she was fine as, at her age, there was not much point in planning any future and at that phrase 'at my age', Patricia became annoyed and reminded her that she was two years older than her and what message was that giving? What should the two of them do? Wait for death? she tried to keep the tone light as she thought the whole discussion was absurd and had to do more with Patricia's own anxiety of death rather than anything else and she would agree, say yes, it was possible she was waiting for death. After all that was what everyone was waiting for. And Patricia said that nevertheless they had to occupy themselves with something while they were waiting, even if it was just to pass the time. Well, she was about to attend a pâtisserie course and she was continuing to teach piano. And at that point Patricia would ask whether she had any plans for a relationship. She knew, of course, that was what Patricia had in mind all along and that was the point of her questions and she would tell her that she had no plans to rush into anything, that she was still in mourning and that she needed to take things slowly. And Patricia would frown and say that, at this rate, she would be in a wheelchair before she decided to act. And then Patricia would remind her that she had complained about the lack of physical intimacy in her life. That wasn't quite true. What she missed was having a face on the pillow next to hers, someone to hug, someone to exchange a few words with when she was in bed and the lights were out. It was true she missed Bill's presence in their bed. She didn't miss sex. They had hardly had any in the last ten years. There was always her vibrator. But she didn't say that. What she did say is that she had to be patient and that something might happen, or it might not. She didn't mind either way. The word patient would send Patricia on a tirade. 'Patient? Patient?' She would repeat the word and say that she sounded as if she were waiting for a man to return from the Crusades. 'Not you,' Patricia would say, she remembers, 'not you, Claire Meadows, you who were arrested at Greenham, you who spent the night in a police cell, with five other dangerous reprobates, including one Patricia Smith.' And they would both laugh, and she would add that 'yes, it's true, that Patricia Smith was without a doubt a dangerous influence.' And then Patricia would tell her not to forget how many times they had camped there. No, she couldn't forget that. Bill was unhappy about her going there, even though she never stayed more than two nights in a row and there was always food ready for him when he returned to the empty house. But when she was arrested, he said enough was enough and she felt that he was speaking like a parent to a little child who had been naughty. And she told him that. She surprised herself by answering back like that. He said he was worried about the scandal. He didn't want to have a wife with a criminal record. It wasn't good for his reputation. She accepted the point but later she realised that his objection had nothing to do with that. He simply wanted her to be at home. He loved her, he said, and she knew that. And that was the first time he called her his 'little, wild Claire'.

She remembers asking Patricia why she was referring to Greenham Common as she didn't understand what their political activism in the past had to do with her love life as a widow. A cue for Patricia to get into her role in earnest: she would stand up and raise an arm as if she were making a speech and say that feminism was not just about politics, or about equal pay, or sharing housework and childcare; 'feminism, let us not forget,' she would declare while waving her finger, 'feminism is also about a woman's right to sexuality, a woman's right to express her desires.' Once, they were in the park when the scene was enacted for the umpteenth time and she remembers looking around nervously to see if anyone could hear it. And then she would tell Patricia that she expresses her desires and that she wasn't shy, but she just didn't think she needed a man, certainly not at that stage in her life. And Patricia would say that perhaps she needed a woman and she would respond that was possible, but that would not be the end of the topic for the day. Patricia would proceed to tell her that she was a very attractive woman and that she should be having fun and that many men would give their right arm to be with someone like her. And she would then ask about why it was better to have a man with no right arm and Patricia would pretend that she was losing her patience. The fact is, Patricia would say, she needed someone wonderful. It always amazed her how despite a lifetime of disastrous relationships, starting with a good-for-nothing husband who took off after their second daughter was born, and followed by a whole army of unsuitable dates, Patricia never lost faith in men. Eventually, Patricia did persuade her to register with three dating agencies, but it was only after Jon had appeared and disappeared. She had a few dozen responses and maintained correspondence with some of the men. She thought that most of them sounded weird, but she wouldn't say that now. Perhaps she was naïve, certainly inexperienced. If there is one thing she has learned, it is that, when it comes to sexuality, there is nothing that can be called weird. Unless it's criminal. Unless it is not consented to. There was one man, how funny she has not thought of him until just now, who told her he had bought one of those silicone dolls for sex but could not get excited without the real thing. He needed a woman to get him going and then he would return to the doll to finish the business. What did he think was in it for the woman? But perhaps none of that was true. She thought that some of the advertisers were there to shock, to create the impression of something unusual, possibly intriguing, and therefore attractive. She felt that there were also those who were there for the sake of writing. Probably failed writers who had found an outlet for their fantasies.

She makes a cup of coffee. Drinks two glasses of water. Always drink a lot of water. Good for the skin, for the digestion, for the kidneys. She has been doing it all her life. And eating water. Eating water, she wondered when she first heard it from a young beautician at a Barbican salon. Yes, cucumbers, melons. She eats cucumbers. Lots of them. Melons are too sweet.

She unrolls a yoga mat and starts her exercises. Warm up the body first. Then press ups. Slow these days. Everything is qualified with 'these days'. A roller. Twenty rolls up and down. And then the dumbbells to tone her upper arms, or at least try to. But it's her skin, the skin that has lost its elasticity and there seems to be too much of it, crumpled and wrinkled. And the spots on her skin; people used to say they were age spots but she developed them in her mid-thirties. Sun damage, a dermatologist told her. The price she paid for sunbathing, always hoping to have a darker skin. She used to find dark people more attractive. Asians and Africans.

She is rolling up the mat when her telephone rings, and it is Gabriel and he says that there has been a change of plan and that the two of them will be with her in an hour. Nothing to worry about, just to let her know they will be there much earlier than agreed.

She takes a shower, instinctively avoiding the reflection of her body in the mirror, still slim but wobbly, lined, misshapen. Despite the exercise, forty years of daily exercise, she looks like a half-filled bag of bones. No one would desire her now. She was never beautiful, no, she didn't think she was, certainly not in any conventional sense but as she aged, she kept her figure and she became good-looking, or that's what people kept telling her. She knew she looked well only in comparison to most women of her age who have let themselves go. But what matters is that she is alive, and her mental faculties are still sound, for the time being at least. She will wear black trousers, neat black trousers and a white shirt. Always flattering, if anything is flattering on her these days. French. French elegance, that's what she has always been striving for. Always effective. The simplicity of it. Ageing means that one has to take more care. No scruffy, messy look. Has she ever embraced her age? Not really. She certainly hasn't aged gracefully, but what does that mean? Wearing baggy dresses, flat shoes. No that's not her. Her hair is no longer dyed. She had it cut the other day, a neat cut. It is too thin, too wispy to be worn long. When she washes it, and applies a great deal of conditioner, it keeps its lustre for a day or two. So many limitations of body and mind. She examines her face. She stares into her eyes. They are still blue, as blue as when she started school and the teacher used to call her 'forget-me-not'. How long ago that was. Is anyone still alive from her first class? Behind the map of lines, she can see the little girl. How the core, the core of the face, and the core of our thinking self, remain the same. The same but obscured by the patina of age, the detritus of living. The mask of age is what others see. Make-up. She needs make-up. She works slowly with a great deal of light. Oily foundation. Always oily these days. Eyebrows, she has to define her non-existent eyebrows. All that senseless plucking in her youth. Women of advanced age tend to overdo the make-up. Every day she reminds herself to use it sparely. The other day at the baker's, she saw a woman, definitely younger than her, probably in her early eighties, with a blush on her cheeks that looked as if she had stuck on two red stickers, that's how defined the edges were. Should she have mentioned it to her, helped her? No, what would have been the point? The woman probably had a weak sight and would have thought she looked fine. Who cares what anyone else thinks if the woman thought she looked well? And then she is ready. She checks the cake and takes it out of the fridge, and she is pleased that the glazing is still shiny. She places the candles next to the cake carry-box. She sits down in the lounge and turns on the radio. She recognises the *Great Fugue*, the music she has always associated with failure and death and her instinct is to turn it off but the beauty of Beethoven's composition compels her to listen and she waits for just one more movement, followed by another and then it is finished. But no, she tells herself, her mood hasn't changed. She is going to a party. A celebration of life. Joy. She smiles. Yes, she is going to a party.

A text arrives from Zach. They are parking. Both of them. It was supposed to have been only Zach. Wasn't Gabriel meant to go straight to the home because he was being interviewed by a journalist? But even better, the two of them together. One of them can read to her. She can see Eliot's poems on the shelf in front of her. And then the bell rings and she hears the key in the lock and the voices of the men. They kiss her, both of them.

'The cake is in the kitchen,' she says 'but is there time for a poem? "Prufrock"; something makes me think I would love to hear "Prufrock" before we leave.'

Zach looks at Gabriel. Gabriel does not say anything. And then Zach says, 'there is no party.'

'There is no party?'

'Martin died this morning.' She stares ahead. Her mind is empty. Is she surprised? How suddenly it happened. But what's sudden about death at one hundred and two? Martin died on his birthday. How perfect. Martin's surprise. Martin's surprise to them all.

Zach hugs her and Gabriel takes her hand and holds it. They sit in silence. And then she asks how it happened. And Zach says Martin died in his sleep. Early this morning. In his sleep. Now it's her turn to say she would like to go like that. Yes, it's her turn, but she doesn't say it.

She remembers when she was thirteen and her grandmother died, the only grandparent she had known and she was sitting in a taxi with her father as he was going around making the funeral arrangements. He said that his mother had fulfilled her role. 'Her work was finished.' Her work? Her role in life. Her role? Yes, she had given birth to him. She had raised him. He was independent. 'She had no more work to do.' Her father spoke as if his mother was just a set of cells, no more than a biological entity programmed to procreate. 'Yes,' he said, 'that's what we are. In the story of the world, in the great evolution, that's all we are.' And now she wonders what role Martin fulfilled. He wrote sixty plus detective novels. He gave pleasure to his readers. But biologically, he was a failure. He didn't reproduce. And yet he used the world's resources and used them for one hundred and two years. In biological terms, he was a waste. And what about her? The same with her. She didn't reproduce. But the two of them did other things. Martin had a gift for friendship. For friendship with her, hardly with a multitude. She hopes she was a good friend to him. And to Patricia. And she has helped Zach find happiness. And Gabriel. That's a lot. And she loved Bill. And she loved Hal. And she was loved back. That's more than most people achieve.

Martin is dead, but they haven't done his music list for the funeral. She will have to do it alone and the responsibility makes her anxious. And what about the cake? She thinks about Martin and images flash in front of her eyes and it strikes her for the first time that there was a certain detached sadness about him all throughout his life. A sadness with no cause. A sadness that she never thought about until now. Now, when there is no more time to do anything about it. And she remembers other deaths. She remembers the death of Bill and her regrets that they didn't have more time to do things together after he retired. And the pills. The pills she gave him; did they kill him? And the relief that evening, relief that she was free, relief mixed with fear. And her lie, her lie to the police that Bill was lying on the sofa and that she had tried to give him the kiss of life and he had slipped onto the floor. And she remembers the death of Hal and she wishes she had been able to see him when he knew he was dying and she wishes she could have held his hand. But she knows there is something pointless, ridiculous about such thoughts. When we live, time marches on, past all our good intentions. When someone dies, and when there is no more time, the good intentions resurface. But they are no longer intentions. They morph into regrets. We become aware of all those things we could have done, all those words we could have said. All that is left is regrets, pointless regrets. And then she remembers a French village on the Canal du Midi where Bill and she had a holiday once and where the church bells rang at each hour and each half hour. But there were two other types of peal: a slow one announcing the death of a resident and a quick one for the birth of a new one and she remembers thinking how death was slow, as if the person dragged their feet and didn't wish to leave and the rapid sequence of bells suggested that the baby was impatient to join the world. Dragging their feet or running, it seems to her it is always too late. She was too late, too late with friends. Too late with her lovers.

And then she asks Zach to read 'Prufrock' and he does and his voice trembles and by the time he reads 'I have heard the mermaids singing, each to each. /I do not think that they will sing to me', they all have tears in their eyes, tears for Prufrock, tears for Martin, tears for themselves. And it occurs to her that whenever we cry after the death of those we knew and loved, we cry for ourselves, like mourners at a Catholic funeral when, once the coffin has been lowered into the earth, the priest asks them to say a prayer for the next one among them. Zach and Gabriel stay late into the night and they have supper together and they drink wine and they cut the cake. But they do not light the candles since the birthday boy is no longer around to make a wish. And they talk about Martin's birthday last year and the one before that, and the one before that. And she remembers to bring out the photographs from all the seventy years that she has made cakes for Martin. The photographs that are a form of transport, a sign of absence. Martin's absence. And she asks Gabriel whether there could be a book there and he says he likes the idea and he will think about it. And she tells them that she would like them to take her to Florence. She wants to see Leonardo's 'Magi' again. And Zach and Gabriel look at their diaries and they pencil in a week in March when they could both go, a month before Gabriel's new novel is published. And she thinks that this time there will be no postcards to send, the three postcards they used to send to Martin every day. They will not be sending postcards but everything else will be the same. She will travel to Florence with her son and his partner.

And she is tired, and she wants to sleep, and Zach and Gabriel leave. She lies in bed and she switches off the light. She remembers the full moon, a large, luminescent, paper cut-out, collaged against the dark sky. Fuliginous sky. She remembers the full moon. Did she dream about the moon? Or does she remember it?

She remembers. Yes.

ACKNOWLEDGEMENTS

THANK YOU TO Peter, my first reader, for his continual support.

Thank you to my friends Marilyn Gregory and Fiona Jones for their helpful comments.

Thank you to Anna Burns for our conversations.

Thank you to Anthony Rudolf for his kindness and encouragement.

Thank you to Salt for believing in me, once again.

This book has been typeset by
SALT PUBLISHING LIMITED
using Neacademia, a font designed by Sergei Egorov for the Rosetta Type Foundry in the Czechia. It has been manufactured using Holmen Book Cream 65gsm paper, and printed and bound by Clays Limited in Bungay, Suffolk, Great Britain.

If you enjoyed this book, do please leave a review on Amazon, Goodreads and your favourite bookstore website.

CROMER
GREAT BRITAIN
MMXXIV